Bartholomew's Passage

Bartholomew's Passage

A Family Story for Advent

Arnold Ytreeide

Kregel
Publications

For maps, drawings, a reading quiz, and other special features, visit www.JothamsJourney.com.

Library of Congress Cataloging-in-Publication Data
Ytreeide, Arnold
Bartholomew's passage : a family story for Advent / Arnold Ytreeide.
    p. cm.
Originally published: Ann Arbor, Mich.: Vine Books, © 2002.
1. Advent—Prayers and devotions. 2. Family—Prayers and devotions. I. Title.
BV40.Y865   2009   242'.332—dc22   2009020302

ISBN 978-0-8254-4173-8

For Elsie—
My wife
My companion
My friend

A Story for Advent

Stir us up, O Lord, to make ready for your only-begotten Son. May we be able to serve you with purity of soul through the coming of him who lives and reigns.

Advent Prayer

Advent. *Adventus. Ecce advenit Dominator Dominus.* Behold, the Lord, the Ruler, is come. Reaching back two millennia to the birth of the Christ child and forward to his reign on earth, the tradition of Advent is a threefold celebration of the birth of Jesus, his eventual second coming to earth, and his continued presence in our lives here and now. God in our past, God in our future, God in our present.

Advent. It started with people going hungry to purify themselves and prepare themselves for holy living. A *fast*, we call it, and such a fast was ordered by the Council of Saragossa in A.D. 381. For three weeks before Epiphany (a feast in January celebrating the divine revelation of Jesus to the gentile Magi), the people were to prepare themselves by fasting and praying. The tradition spread to France in 581 by decree of the Council of Macon, and to Rome and beyond thereafter. Gregory the First refined the season to its present form in about 600 when he declared that it should start the fourth Sunday before Christmas.

Fasting is no longer a part of Advent in most homes and churches (though it wouldn't be a bad idea). For us, Advent means taking time each day, for the three or four weeks before Christmas, to center our thoughts on Truth Incarnate lying in a feeding trough in Bethlehem.

It's a time of worship, a time of reflection, a time of focus, and a time of family communion. In the midst of December's commotion and stress, Advent is a few moments to stop, catch your breath, and renew your strength from the only One who can provide true strength.

Bartholomew's Passage is one tool you can use to implement a time of Advent in your family—whether yours is a traditional family structure, or one of the many combinations of fathers and mothers, stepparents and grandparents, and guardians and children that make up today's families. You can use this story during Advent even if your family is just you.

Set aside a few minutes each day, beginning the fourth Sunday before Christmas (see the chart in the back of the book) to light the Advent candles, read the *Bartholomew* story and devotional for that day, and pray together. You can also use an Advent calendar (see "Advent Customs"), sing a favorite Christ-centered carol (Frosty's a nice guy but has no place in Advent), and have a time of family sharing.

In our family we set aside fifteen minutes each night before the youngest child goes to bed. Our Advent wreath has a traditional place on a table next to the living room reading chair. The children take turns lighting the candles and reading all the open windows of the Advent calendar, and then adding that day's reading at the end. By the light of the Advent candles I read the last few lines of the previous day's Bartholomew story, then go on to to-day's story and devotion.

Afterward my wife leads in prayer as we all hold hands. We close by singing one verse of a carol. Then the youngest child lights her own "bedside" candle from the Advent candles and makes her way to bed by candlelight. (This is only for children who are old enough to know how to use a candle safely.) Even when work or visiting takes us out of town, we carry *Bartholomew's Passage* and a candle with us and keep our Advent tradition. Sometimes we even get to share our tradition with those we are visiting.

Simple, short, spiritual. A wonderful way to keep the shopping, traffic, rehearsals, concerts, parties, and all the other preparations of December in balance with the reality of God in our lives—past, present, and future.

Advent. *Adventus. Ecce advenit Dominator Dominus.* Behold, the Lord, the Ruler, is come. May God richly bless you and your family as you prepare to celebrate the birth of Christ!

Advent Customs

Advent itself is simply a time set apart for spiritual preparation. But most people associate the word *Advent* with various traditions and customs that have grown up around Christmas in many of the world's cultures. Early in history these customs took the forms of fasts and feasts. Today, they most often take the form of candles, wreaths, and calendars.

Most churches and families use Advent candles to celebrate the season. Five are used in all, one for each week of Advent and a fifth for Christmas Day. The first, second, and fourth candles are violet, symbolizing penitence. The third is pink, symbolizing joy, and the Christmas Day candle is white, symbolizing the purity of Christ.

Advent candles are usually part of an Advent wreath. While some traditions hang the wreath, it is most commonly used flat, on a table. The circle of the wreath represents the hope of eternal life we have through Christ. The circle itself is made of evergreen branches, symbolizing the abundant life Jesus promised us here and now. The first four candles are positioned along the outside ring of the wreath, and the fifth is placed in the center.

Some traditions use a slanted board instead of a wreath to hold the candles. The board is about four inches by twelve, and raised six inches on one end. Four holes are drilled along the length of the board for the first four candles, and the fifth candle is placed at the top.

Another candle tradition uses one candle for each day of Advent. Any color of candle can be used, but the Sunday candles are usually of a special design and color. The candles can be placed either along a mantel or in holes drilled in a log. Each night during devotions one more candle is lit. By Christmas Day, the candles give bright testimony to and reminder of the evenings of devotion you've spent together as a family.

Advent calendars are popular with children and teach them the Christmas story in an active way. Also called an "Advent house," the calendar is shaped like a house, with a window for each day of Advent. Behind each window is a small portion of the Christmas story (usually from the book of Luke). Each night the family reads the story from these windows, ending with the window for that day.

A Note to Parents: Jesus was not born in an amusement park or religious retreat. He was born into a world of sin, darkness, and death. Indeed, His own birth caused the death of hundreds of male children as Herod sought to kill the new King. So it is not the intent of *Bartholomew's Passage* to present a heavenlike world where everyone lives in purity and harmony. While the story is fun and adventurous and has the most happy of endings, it does take place in the real world: there is greed, there is cruelty, there is death. The point is not to cover up the dark side of life but rather to show how the love of God and His Son Jesus Christ is the *light* of our lives.

Most children over the age of seven have been exposed to far worse violence in movies, TV, and cartoons than you'll find in this story. However, if your children are younger than seven, or are particularly sensitive, I suggest you preview each day's reading so that you might skip or summarize the few more tragic parts. You may also want to talk with your children about the events in the story, to help them understand that sometimes bad things happen to people, but that you and God are there to love them and protect them. That is, after all, the reason God sent His Son to us in the first place!

In any event, it is my sincere hope and prayer that you and God together can use this story to teach your children just how much God loves them and how close He is to us, even in times of tragedy.

Especially in times of tragedy.

May God richly bless your Advent time together!

The Storm

Light the first violet candle.

N o!" The voice of the butcher was low and gruff as he chopped another rib with a swing of his cleaver. Bartholomew ducked the splatters of blood that flew every which way, then looked up at the angry face above him. .

"Aw, *please*, Joab!" he pleaded. "It's just *perfect!*"

Joab slammed the cleaver between two more ribs and said, "That's exactly why I won't give it to you! Such a thing will draw a handsome price from some traveling prince or the like."

Bartholomew eyed the ram's horn again, allowing his gaze to travel the circles of its coil, then moved slowly around the table. He climbed up on a stool and leaned forward until he was inches from Joab's ear. "I have Persian tea," he whispered temptingly.

Joab's cleaver stopped in midswing and he turned to Bartholomew. "You have no such thing!"

With that, Bartholomew pulled a small leather bag from his tunic and swung it back and forth under Joab's nose. "A whole bag of Persian tea for one little ram's horn," he taunted. "A very good trade, I should think."

Joab's nose twitched as he watched the bag, transfixed. "And how did you come by such a treasure?" he asked.

Bartholomew smiled. "Oh, I happened upon a Persian caravan searching the desert for something or other, and they were most happy to be supplied with some fresh redfish."

Joab continued watching the bag, smelling the aroma of the tea, imagining its flavor wrapping itself around his tongue. Finally he could stand it no more. With his free hand he swiped the bag from Bartholomew's hand and stuck it inside his tunic. "Done!" he said.

With a grin, Bartholomew jumped off the stool, grabbed the ram's horn and the ribs his mother had sent him for, and headed for the door. "A good trade, Joab!" he called out as he left. Joab just scratched his chin and wondered if he had yet again been fleeced by the ten-year-old boy.

Once outside, Bartholomew ran down the street, laughing into the sunshine. The streets of Taricheae were narrow, but the sun was straight overhead and shone brightly on the houses and shops of stone. He would take the ram's horn, he had decided, and carve it into a horn for signaling. Then he would trade it for a fine tunic the size of a man, and finally trade *that* to Jacob for the little boat the old boat builder was keeping for him. *It will all work out perfectly*, he thought. *Just the way I planned.*

But first, he had to get the ribs home to his mother. It would be good to have some deer meat for a change. When your father's a fisherman, that pretty much determines what you eat most of the time.

Bartholomew ran down the streets of hard-packed dirt, mostly because he ran everywhere. He passed his friend Marakin, owner of the copper stand, and his friend Baldanod, owner of the cloth stand, and his friend Jesselram, owner of the cheese stand, and all his other friends at all the other stands throughout the small town. Bartholomew was, in fact, friends with most everyone in the village, including the seagulls that constantly circled overhead.

Of course, he had friends his own age too, and he stopped long enough to play a round of King's Ransom with three of them. He won.

Finally Bartholomew reached his home, two stories tall with a nice big roof perfect for sleeping on warm summer nights such as this was sure to be. It was built shoulder-to-shoulder with rows of other such houses on a side street wider than most. When he ran through the door, his mother was just kneading some bread dough.

"Did you get my ribs?" she called out when she saw her son.

"I think your ribs are right where they've always been!" Bartholomew answered with a grin.

His mother laughed. She had seven children, and loved them all with buckets full of love, but Bartholomew could always make her laugh.

"Well then, perhaps you brought me the ribs of a *deer*?" she asked, playing along.

"Ah, that I did!" Bartholomew said, and plunked the package down on the table.

"And did you also give Hannah the money for the corn?"

"Yes, Mother."

"And you asked Nimmock about your reading lessons?"

"Yes, Mother."

"Well then," she said, "I think you've done all the things a mother can expect of her son. Why don't you go down and meet your father?"

Bartholomew grinned. "I guess if you're going to *make* me," he said, knowing full well that *she* knew full well that going down to the sea was about his most favorite thing in the world to do. "But first I must put this away," he said, holding up the ram's horn.

"And where did you find such a beautiful horn?" his mother asked.

"I traded Joab for it."

Bartholomew's mother just shook her head, still smiling. "I swear, child, that you could talk the Evil One himself into being good!"

Bartholomew grinned again, then headed up the narrow stairway of stone. The smoke from his mother's cook fire was also climbing the stairs, and the smell of baking bread made his stomach feel hungry. Dinner would be a special event on this night. Of course, Bartholomew felt that most any meal was a special event.

In the upstairs room, Bartholomew's three sisters were sewing cloth to make new bed-covers and talking so much they sounded like a flock of cackling geese. But as soon as Bartholomew stuck his head up through the floor, their cackling stopped, replaced by giggling.

Bartholomew didn't understand girls at all. It seemed as if they were always talking about nothing or giggling about nothing or pouting over nothing. The older boys in the town seemed to think his sisters were very special, but Bartholomew couldn't figure out why. He loved them, of course, and even sort of *liked* them sometimes. But mostly he just couldn't figure them out.

The three girls watched Bartholomew cross the room and climb the wooden ladder. As soon as his head popped through the hole in the ceiling that led to the roof, he heard them start jabbering again. He climbed out on the roof and went to the far corner, where he could look out over the whole town and see everything, and where he kept his sleeping mat during the summer. Taking his bedcover, he gently wrapped the ram's horn in it.

The building next door had a funny kind of roof, and was a few feet taller than Bartholomew's house. He had long ago discovered a few loose boards on the end of the roof, just above the place where he rolled out his bed. So now he climbed up on the wall of his own house and pulled back the boards that led to his secret hiding place. Here the ram's horn would be safe, he knew, just a few feet from where his father and mother slept.

His task done, Bartholomew climbed back down the ladder, across the room where his sisters giggled silently, down the staircase of stone, past the cook fire where his mother smiled at him as she kneaded dough, and out the front door. Most days his father and brothers wouldn't return home until sunset, but this was *Friday*, the beginning of the *Sabbath*, the special day set aside each week to honor God. From sundown tonight until sundown the next night, Bartholomew's family would do no work and would listen to his father tell stories of Noah and Abraham and Gideon and David—and his father's favorite stories about the coming Messiah.

Bartholomew ran down the narrow, sun-filled streets, passing his friend Elazra, who owned the iron shop, and his friend Uvira, who owned the spices shop, and his friend Tulmara, who owned the lamp-oil shop, and downhill all the way to the edge of the Sea of Galilee, which was just about his favorite place in the world. Squinting against the sunlight that bounced off the glassy water, Bartholomew stared out at the lake until he could make out his father's boat headed for shore.

Running past the fishing boats that had already landed, Bartholomew skirted nets the size of houses and fishermen hauling bucket-loads of fish and men haggling over the price of their catch, until he got to the place where his father always landed his boat, just as his father arrived.

"Father! Father!" Bartholomew called, waving. His father raised his hand in greeting, then jumped over the side of the boat as it neared the shore. Bartholomew's three brothers pushed the boat with their oars as his father pulled it by the bow. Bartholomew sloshed out into the water, grabbed the rope tied to the front of the boat, and pulled as if he could beach the craft all by himself.

"Did you get anything?" Bartholomew asked excitedly. Fishing was the life of their small family, he knew. A good catch meant easy times, a poor catch meant smaller meals and no new clothes.

"It was a fine catch today," Bartholomew's father said with a grin. "Perhaps the largest in many months!" Bartholomew smiled. Times had been very good lately, and a catch this size would only make things better.

Bartholomew hopped on the boat and helped his father and brothers unload the fish. He teased his brothers about smelling like the fish they were unloading, so, with a laugh, they tossed Bartholomew off the end of the boat and into the water. Bartholomew got the last laugh, though, when he tightened himself into a ball as he flew through the air so he'd make a bigger splash. It worked, and his brothers got almost as wet as Bartholomew. But they pulled him out, still laughing and joking, and together they got the boat unloaded in a very short time.

"Bartholomew, you may stay and dry the nets while we take the fish into town," his father said. This made Bartholomew very happy, since he'd rather be around the lake and the boats than in town any day of the week.

The other men of his family now gone, Bartholomew set to work spreading the nets out to dry. They were made of a thick brown rope and weighed about as much as a horse, it seemed, but by tugging and pulling on first one side and then the other, Bartholomew was able to get all the nets out of the boat and drying before the sun had traveled very far toward the horizon. As he worked, he thought about the lessons he would soon start. He would learn to read and would study the Torah—the holy book of God—just like his older brothers.

Bartholomew was just pulling the last corner of the last net into place when he noticed the thunder. He had better hurry home, he realized. A storm could come up faster than a person could think on Galilee. The whole lake could be as calm as a sleeping baby, then you could be in the middle of a storm before you knew what was happening. Sunshine one minute, wind and rain the next.

Bartholomew pulled harder, looking toward the horizon over the sea. *No clouds*, he thought. But that doesn't mean anything. He could hear the thunder, and that meant a storm.

But then Bartholomew noticed that the thunder wasn't coming from the lake; it was coming from the hills behind the village. At the same moment he noticed that the other fishermen, pulling and tugging at their own nets, had stopped working and were looking toward town. Some of them seemed puzzled, others worried, but Bartholomew saw that the smartest of the fishermen he knew were scared. Suddenly several of the men grabbed their oars and knives and hooks and anything else they could find and started running toward town. The others seemed to realize what was happening and did the same, leaving Bartholomew all alone on the beach.

It was then that Bartholomew heard the first of the screams.

Storms come and storms go, and usually they're easily weathered by closing the doors and windows. But every once in a while there comes a storm that is stronger than doors, a storm that can break through the windows and invade every corner of a home.

It's pretty easy to weather the average storms of flat tires, mild colds, and fights with friends. But what about when those big storms hit, when life is in chaos and nothing is the same as it used to be? What do we do then? How do we survive?

That's one of the reasons God sent Jesus to us as His personal ambassador. He wanted to let us know that He is real, that He is with us, and that He cares. That's why Jesus spoke about the foolishness of building our lives on the sandy ground of earthly desires: money, popularity, power, and lots of "things." It's why He told us to build instead on the solid rock of God's unfailing love.

Bartholomew has lived through times when his father's catch wasn't quite enough to feed the family and through times when the catch was so big they had an easy life. Whether in times of plenty or times of want, he has always known the security of his friends and family and the little town he loves. But is he ready for the storm on his horizon?

Are *we* ready for the storms in *our* future?

Advent is a time when we can concentrate on building a better relationship with God. It's a time when we can put aside thoughts of Christmas gifts to focus on the *original* gift of Christmas. It's a time when we can allow God's love to become so real to us that we can weather even the worst of life's storms.

May God be with you and reveal Himself to you, as you spend these few minutes with Him each day this Advent!

Tidal Wave

Light the first violet candle.

Bartholomew dropped the net he was holding and ran toward the town. As he came around the last of the seaside buildings he could see smoke rising from the far side of town. A fire, he now realized. Some big building had caught fire, and all the men were rushing to put it out, just as they always did. When you live in a small town, after all, everyone must pitch in.

Wanting to do his part, Bartholomew continued running up the narrow streets. The smoke had spread by now and seemed to be coming from everywhere, making it hard to know where the fire really was. A lot of women and children were running past him, trying to get away from the flames. Many of them were screaming and holding their babies tightly. But Bartholomew knew that a man doesn't run away from such a thing; he faces it head-on and works with the other men to take care of it.

With all the commotion and confusion, Bartholomew really didn't know which way to go, so he decided to climb up high to get a better view. He was just passing the perfume shop owned by his friend Dothan, and he knew Dothan wouldn't mind his trespassing. With the speed of a rabbit he climbed the narrow stone staircase on the outside of the building and up onto the roof where Dothan dried the leaves of fragrant plants. He looked out over the city and gasped: there wasn't just one fire but many!

Bartholomew's mother had taught him to count things on his fingers, but it would take the fingers of *ten* men to count all these fires. How would they ever put them all out?

But then Bartholomew raised his eyes above the fires, to the hills on the other side of town. And there, through the smoke, he saw a sight that burned forever into his memory, a sight that struck fear in the heart of every Jew, no matter how strong or how brave.

He saw Romans.

The thunder he'd heard hadn't been a storm at all, nor the roar of the fire, he now realized. It had been the hooves of dozens of horses, pounding out an angry advance. They covered the hills, Bartholomew saw, surrounding the town on all three sides. He saw them charging through every gate in the city wall, saw them storming through the streets on the outer edge of town.

And then he saw them killing.

With swords and clubs and the feet of their horses, the Romans were striking and stomping anyone who got in their way. People would run one way to flee from one squad of soldiers only to run into another.

All these sights paralyzed Bartholomew, so that he couldn't think or move or even breathe for what seemed like an hour. Finally, a scream closer than the rest broke through his trance and brought just one thought to his mind—*My family*—and then he raced back down the narrow stone staircase.

Panic had swept through the people of Bartholomew's town like the fires that were racing through the buildings. Everyone was trying to push in a different direction because no one knew which direction led to safety. People who had been friends for years now kicked and shoved each other in a terrible battle to survive.

The sound of horses' hooves was closer now—all around, it seemed to Bartholomew. Twice he turned a corner to run blindly into a Roman foot soldier, and twice he managed to jump away before the soldier could react. On his hands and knees, he fought his way between the legs of friends and neighbors who were fighting each other to escape the Roman swords. Finally, covered with dirt and sweat—and blood!—Bartholomew reached his home. He ran inside, yelling for his mother and father.

The house was empty.

But worse than that, the house had been ransacked. The table where his mother had been kneading bread just an hour before was upside-down, broken, the bread dough and flour ground into the floor. Water jars lay smashed and empty; bedrolls and tunics had been thrown everywhere.

Crying now, his insides feeling like a swarm of angry bees, Bartholomew climbed the stairway of stone to the top floor of their house. His sisters no longer sat sewing their bed-covers and giggling. Quickly Bartholomew climbed the wooden ladder and saw that the roof, too, was abandoned.

The screams in the street were just below him now, and Bartholomew looked over the edge to see squads of Romans coming from every direction. His only thought now to survive, he quickly crawled into his secret place, the hole in the wall where his house met the next house, and pulled closed the boards that some carpenter had put there long ago. He wrapped his arms tightly around his head to block out the screams, but nothing could. Sobbing as silently as he could, he trembled and shook and willed the evil to go away.

A few hours later the screams had stopped. Smoke still filled every breath he took, but Bartholomew could no longer hear what was happening outside. The sun was setting, he could tell from the way the light came through the boards, and for a moment he thought he really should be preparing for the Sabbath. But then he realized there would be no Sabbath on this night. And maybe never again.

Bartholomew was just thinking these thoughts when suddenly the boards next to him shattered in an explosion of splinters. The red light of the setting sun jabbed at his eyes, making him squint even as he jumped in fear. Then he felt a hand, as rough as a fisher-man's and ten times the size of his own, clamp around his throat and pull him out into the air. Dangling three feet above the roof, Bartholomew stared into the black eyes of a Roman soldier dressed in dirty and bloody capes of gold.

"Found another one!" the soldier yelled over his shoulder to some unseen companion. And somehow, somehow, Bartholomew knew that his life would never be the same again.

Storms come and storms go, but every once in a while comes a storm so big . . .

Is Bartholomew ready for the storm that has struck? Are *we* ready for the times that test us, tempt us, rip away the life we know and the ones we love?

We *can* be. God has promised us all His strength and all His love. He showed us, through

Jesus, how to face the most terrible moments in life and still emerge victorious. We can't do it on our own strength, of course. And we can't do it by turning to Him only when we want something. We *prepare* ourselves by purposely building a relationship with *Him*, trying to be the person He wants us to be, doing our best to love others as unselfishly as He loves us.

Building such a relationship with God is not an easy thing to do. But God took the first giant step by sending Jesus to teach us and demonstrate love for us. No, it's not an easy thing to do, but when we finally decide to let go of our pride and our ego and our selfishness, and allow God to teach us how to love, then we are ready for both the wonderful, happy times of life and the terrible storms as well.

"I will never leave you or forsake you," God said. That's a promise you can count on during this Advent season—and every day for the rest of your life.

Caesarea

Light the first violet candle.

The whip cracked again and Bartholomew jumped. Somewhere on the road behind him a man screamed. Bartholomew turned his head slightly to sneak a peek back through the men, women, and children trudging up the road and saw that it was his friend, Baldanod, owner of the cloth stand. Baldanod was feeling the sting of the whip.

Once again Bartholomew thought about the terrible events of the day before. After the Roman had found him hiding, Bartholomew had been taken to the center of town, to the Court of Elders, where people bought and sold things and men sat arguing about the Torah or the laws or the weather.

Or the Romans.

It was usually a happy place, where Bartholomew visited with his old friends and talked his way into new friendships. But yesterday the court was not a happy place at all. Everyone in the village—everyone left alive, that is—had been herded there like sheep, guarded by more Roman soldiers than Bartholomew had ever seen in one place. Most of the women were crying, some so hard that they couldn't even stand, and most of the men were angry, some so much that they couldn't stop themselves from throwing rocks at the Romans. Friends had to hold them back so they wouldn't be killed.

But some of the *women* were angry, and some of the *men* were crying, and, well, things were just all mixed-up. Of course, during all this, the only thing Bartholomew wanted was to find his family. None of them were in the courtyard—not his father or mother or three sisters or three brothers. *They must have escaped from the city,* Bartholomew thought, *and will be coming back to rescue me at any minute.*

But they didn't.

Through most of the night, which seemed as long as a winter and just as cold, Bartholomew searched, and waited, and cried, and searched some more. His friends tried to comfort him, to tell him everything would be all right, but he could see in their faces that they didn't really believe this. And so he finally huddled in the corner of the street where the forum met the bathhouse and cried away the rest of the night.

Then this morning, without any food or any explanation at all, the Romans had made all the people line up and started them marching this road, up and out of the town, across the fields of Galilee, to a place Bartholomew did not know.

"Bartholomew!" The whisper had come from behind, but Bartholomew couldn't see the face that had spoken it. "Bartholomew!" it came again. This time he turned and saw that it was Joab, the butcher with whom he had traded for the ram's horn. Not daring to speak, Bartholomew answered with his eyes.

"Do you have the ram's horn I gave you?" Joab whispered. Bartholomew wanted to say that Joab hadn't *given* him *any*thing, that he had made an honorable trade for the horn, but instead only shook his head.

"A shame," Joab whispered yet again. "It might have bought freedom for both of us!"

Hearing the crack of the whip and another cry, Bartholomew faced forward again and kept plodding along like all the others. A squall passed, and the cold rain made him shiver. It also made the ground as slick as ox grease, and Bartholomew had trouble making his feet stay where he put them.

Suddenly the line stopped moving, and people up ahead started shouting. Several Romans rode past toward the commotion, and for the first time all day everyone started talking. "Maybe it's a rebellion!" some were saying, or "Maybe the Zealots have attacked!" Bartholomew only thought, *Maybe my family has come to rescue me!* But soon a single tall Roman rode back along the line on a single grey horse, dragging behind him by the foot at the end of a rope a single young man that Bartholomew knew only as Malachim. The boy looked as if he had been trampled by a hundred angry camels, and Bartholomew was pretty sure he was dead. The Roman kept shouting over and over, "This is what happens to troublemakers!"

Bartholomew had never been called a troublemaker, and he decided this was not the time to start. "Rabbi," one of the men from town whispered to the town's religious leader, "wouldn't this be a good time for the Messiah to come?" Bartholomew couldn't see the old, bearded rabbi, but could hear his answer clear enough. "The Messiah will come in His own time," he said, and Bartholomew thought he sounded very sad.

The column started moving again, and Bartholomew decided he'd better keep right in step with those around him, and keep his eyes on the dirt of the road so he wouldn't be branded a troublemaker.

For three days Bartholomew marched with those left alive from his town. He was given only one meal a day, at sunset, and a few sips of water. At night some people would try to escape, but they were always caught and killed. The first night Bartholomew cried himself to sleep thinking about his family, wondering where they were. After that he decided he shouldn't cry anymore. He had to be strong like the other men.

Then, on the afternoon of the third day, the stream of tired and dirty people crested a hill. And when it was Bartholomew's turn at the top, he saw a sight that at any other time would have thrilled him. A great, bluish green sea stretched to the horizon, and on its shore sat a city that looked big enough to hold the whole world. Ships with masts as tall as three buildings waited in the harbor. Camel trains and trader camps surrounded the city wall.

"Caesarea!" someone gasped. But the name meant nothing to Bartholomew. Soon they were entering the fortress, and they were led to a large courtyard. Roman men entered from the other side of the yard. *They look as clean as women, Bartholomew thought, and are dressed in clothes completely useless for work.* Each Roman would point to one or two or three of Bartholomew's friends, then they'd all leave together. He didn't understand what was happening even when he was at the front of the line, or even when a Roman who had a face like a skunk pointed at him and said something to the soldier in charge. Nor did he understand why the soldier told him to go with the skunk man, and so he asked.

The Roman soldier looked at him in shock for a moment, then laughed as if Bartholomew had told some great and funny joke. Then he said five words that changed Bartholomew's life forever. "You're a slave now, boy!" he said.

And then he laughed again.

Sometimes sin keeps us marching down a road we don't want to travel. We *want* to quit being selfish and doing those things which we know displease God and hurt others, but we can't stop ourselves, even when we see others dying spiritually from the same sin. We become slaves to our sin, with seemingly no choice in the matter. Like Bartholomew, we are taken to places we don't want to go and forced to serve a master that we don't even like.

But *un*like Bartholomew, we *do* have a choice. As Paul wrote:

> What a wretched man I am! Who will rescue me from this body of death?
> Thanks be to God—through Jesus Christ our Lord!　　　ROMANS 7:24–25

Paul knew, and *we* can know, that release from the captivity of sin comes only through a day-by-day relationship with the One whose birth we celebrate on Christmas Day. Paul knew, and we can know, both the forgiveness of sin and freedom from its bondage, which Jesus bought for us with His life.

Slave School

Light the first violet candle.

Y ou're a slave now, boy!" the Roman soldier had barked. And with those words Bartholomew's life changed forever. The soldier shoved Bartholomew toward the skunk man and the skunk man jumped back, as if the boy carried some terrible disease. Another man was with the skunk man—a Jew, Bartholomew could tell, dressed in a plain tunic, standing with his head hung low and hands clasped behind his back.

"Hasbah!" the skunk man said to the Jew. "Take this filthy boy!"

"Yes, Master," the Jew said, then he pulled Bartholomew over to stand next to him. To Bartholomew it seemed as if the whole world were tumbling like the dice he used when playing King's Ransom. Everything was all mixed-up, and he felt like he was going to fall, so dizzy was his head. He grabbed Hasbah's arm to hold himself up, but the slave pushed him away and scowled.

Skunk Man chose two others from among the townspeople of Taricheae: the wife of Bartholomew's friend Uvira, and Mordecai, an older boy Bartholomew had never liked much. Then Skunk Man went over to a table, paid the man sitting there some money, and left the courtyard through an arched doorway.

Hasbah pushed Bartholomew toward the same arch and said to all three of the new slaves, "Follow him, and don't be slow!" Just before they went through the archway, Mordecai screamed and fell backward. Bartholomew saw that the older boy had almost stepped into a hole, and he looked to see what had scared him so. Peeking over the edge, he, too, gasped and jumped backward. The pit was more than a good jump across and deep enough to bury an elephant. And covering the bottom from wall to wall was a slithering mass of roiling, coiling snakes.

Bartholomew bumped into Hasbah, who pushed him back toward the hole. The two boy-slaves stared at the snakes while the woman quickly turned her head. Skunk Man came back through the arch, his pure white robes flowing like the wind. He stopped right in front of the three new slaves and looked at them with the devil's eye.

"That's for slaves who try to run away," he said with a nod toward the pit, and his threat was very clear. Skunk Man stared at them, then turned back through the arch. Bartholomew felt a shove in his back and made his feet start shuffling forward through the arch and through the streets of Caesarea, but his mind could see nothing but the pit full of snakes. And that's why he had no idea where he was or how he'd gotten there when the skunk man finally turned into a low doorway of stone. He led the three new slaves down a chilly stone hallway, then through another doorway and out into the sunlight of a courtyard. A dozen slaves were busy baking bread and carving wood and filling water buckets from a well.

Skunk Man stopped and looked at the three again. "You're mine now," he said. "Hasbah will teach you how to serve me." Then he turned and was gone, and Bartholomew felt as if he'd just been locked in a prison—which, he decided, is exactly what had just happened.

And like a jailor, Hasbah slowly took up a whip and tapped its coils into his other hand. "You will sleep in those two rooms there," he said, pointing to two doors at the other end of the court. "You will rise one hour before dawn and may not enter the sleeping quarters again until you finish your work sometime after the master goes to bed. You will eat two meals a day of coosa and have fish or meat once each week."

Bartholomew gagged at the thought of eating coosa, a pasty black squash, and was pretty sure by his look of disgust that Hasbah's own meals were something more appealing. "You will each be given several tasks to perform each day. Do not forget them, and do them well." Hasbah said nothing about the whip in his hand, but Bartholomew knew exactly what it meant.

Then Hasbah called three other slaves over and assigned them to teach the newcomers. Bartholomew was told to go with Darius, a young man who Bartholomew thought should be off somewhere raising a family, instead of slaving for a Roman.

"You're too small to do a man's work," Darius said. "I don't know why they even assigned you to me. I'd pass you off to one of the women if I could." Then he turned and walked away, and Bartholomew wondered if he should follow. Finally he ran to catch up as Darius went through a doorway into the master's personal quarters.

"Keep your eyes on the floor and your hands folded whenever you're in the house," Darius said. "Unless, of course, you're carrying something. Never speak to the master unless he asks you a question, and never go into any room while he's there unless told to do so. Break these rules and you will lose one meal." Darius listed a dozen or two more rules and lots more punishments, each one worse than the former. Then he showed Bartholomew his jobs.

"Each morning you will scrub the floor of the master's bedroom," Darius said, showing Bartholomew a room so beautiful that he imagined it must be straight from heaven. It had tiles in the floor that made a picture of the sun, moon, and stars, and a bed carved of white marble, as white as the skunk man's skin. *Except I'd better stop calling him the skunk man*, Bartholomew thought.

Darius listed twenty-seven tasks that Bartholomew had to do each day, and Bartholomew thought each one of them would take at least an hour. In the days that followed he had to scrub floors and fill lamps and carry firewood and help the women milk the cows and do lots of other jobs that kept him so tired he didn't even have the strength to cry himself to sleep at night. But the worst, absolutely worst job, the one that he hated the most, was emptying the chamber pots each morning—the clay pots the Roman members of the household used for their toilet.

Every moment he was awake, Bartholomew thought about only three things: He thought about escaping, he thought about his parents, and he thought about the Messiah. But escape seemed impossible, so when his brain got tired of thinking about that, his thoughts centered on his parents. *Where were they?* he wondered. *When would his father rescue him? What's taking so long?* Then he would think about his father's face, smiling after a good catch, and about his mother teasing him, and he'd feel lonely all over again. That's when he'd think about the Messiah and how this would be a most excellent time for Him to come and take care of all the Romans.

The only time Bartholomew found anything to be happy about at all was when he got to go into the town. He loved looking at the big sailing ships tied up at the docks, and he loved watching the waves break against the walls of the fortress on a point of land jutting out from the town. He'd watch the seabirds overhead, the waves of the Mediterranean, and the hundreds of people who traveled through the city. Some were dressed in colorful robes, others in shiny fabrics as light as the air, still others in simple tunics like his own.

It was on one of these days, when he was going with Darius to fetch new straw for the master's bed, that Bartholomew spotted his friend Tulmara, who had owned the lamp-oil shop back in Taricheae. "Tulmara! Tulmara!" Bartholomew called, not caring a bit that slaves don't do such things and ignoring Darius's scowl.

Tulmara lifted his eyes at the sound, saw the boy running toward him, then quickly turned away with a glance at a Roman standing nearby. The Roman was busy talking with another man, so Tulmara looked back at Bartholomew and made a face that said, "Go away!" But Bartholomew didn't notice and ran up to his old friend, who looked a lot older these days, if Bartholomew had taken the time to notice.

"Tulmara," Bartholomew said, hugging the man, "it is so good to see a friendly face!"

"Quiet, boy!" the former lamp-oil salesman whispered, trying to push the boy away. "This is not the place for a reunion!"

Bartholomew ignored the warning. "Do you have any news of our village?" he asked.

"No, I have no news!" Tulmara said urgently, pushing Bartholomew away.

Bartholomew started to protest, but just then Darius grabbed him by the neck and dragged him off. "Run away again and I'll have you whipped no matter *how* young you are," he said.

"But, Tulmara," Bartholomew yelled over his shoulder, "what of my parents?"

At this Tulmara looked remarkably distressed and, glancing again at his own master, called back, "Bartholomew, have you not heard?"

An arrow of fear struck Bartholomew in the heart as he called through the crowd, "Heard what?! Tulmara, what do you know?!"

For the first time since Bartholomew had seen him, Tulmara seemed to quit worrying about his master, and turned his gaze fully on the boy who was his friend. And as the distance between them grew, and through the crowds of people that passed between them, Tulmara yelled the words that once again changed Bartholomew's life forever.

"Bartholomew," he called, "your father and mother were shipped to Rome as slaves!"

And at that, not the scolding of Darius, nor the threat of the whip, nor fear of a skunk man could keep Bartholomew's legs from collapsing underneath him. His parents were gone, prisoners, an ocean away on the other side of the world.

And there would be no rescue.

Sometimes tragedies strike that are so terrible it's hard for us to imagine that we can even go on living. They can smother us in grief, making it difficult even to breathe. These things change our lives forever in ways we never wanted or asked for, ways over which we have no control.

Bartholomew has reached just such a moment in his life. Being sold into slavery was bad enough, but to learn that his parents are also slaves and have been sent to what seems like the other side of the world, has taken away all reason to live. Worse still, he has no one to share his grief with, no one he can cry with, no one who loves him.

Grief is a natural result of tragedy. It takes time to express all of our anger and loneliness and frustration. If you refuse to let those emotions out, they eventually become hatred, bitterness, fear, or insecurity. But if you share those emotions with someone and allow yourself to express your grief, God can heal your pain.

Advent is the time when we look forward to celebrating the birth of Jesus. Usually during this time we thank God for His gift of salvation. But Jesus came not only to save us from our sins but to show us just how real and close God is to us. His love can overcome the worst of tragedies if we keep remembering that He truly is in control, no matter what. He is even now with Bartholomew, even if Bartholomew doesn't know it yet. He is even now with us, though we often forget.

The LORD is near to all who call on him, to all who call on him in truth.

PSALM 145:18

May the truth of God's nearness be made real to you this Advent.

Comings and Goings

Light the first violet candle.

Sometime in the middle of the night Bartholomew had fallen asleep. When he awoke it was still dark, and the other men and boys in the room were still sleeping. *It sounds like a herd of slumbering cows*, Bartholomew thought in one small part of his brain. But most of his mind still felt as if it were being crushed between two giant rocks, and his heart felt as flat as the unleavened bread of Passover, which he and the other Jews would not get to celebrate the next week.

Bartholomew had become hysterical at the news of his parents' fate, falling to the ground, wrapping his arms around Darius's ankles, crying like a lamb separated from its mother. Darius had first tried to kick him away, then he had pulled him up by the tunic, dragged him to the stable, filled his arms with hay, and led him home again. Once there, Bartholomew just sat in a corner of the courtyard between a stone wheel used for grinding wheat and a large rack used for beating the dirt from the master's colorful carpets. He didn't finish his work and therefore wasn't allowed to have dinner, but he didn't much care. His world had just been ripped apart as if by a herd of stampeding camels, and he felt as if nothing could ever repair it.

So he cried alone in the dark, each memory of his father and mother lighting a new fire of grief in his heart. He cried through the dark hours, and on through the sunrise, and well into midmorning. At some point, a Roman in the household noticed that her chamber pot hadn't been emptied. All the slaves started blaming all the other slaves, until someone finally dragged Bartholomew out into the courtyard. Hasbah laid him over a bench and took a leather strap to his bottom.

After that Bartholomew dragged himself through the days, doing all his work without any care and without any thought. He didn't even find it unpleasant to empty the chamber pots because you can't find something unpleasant when you really don't care about anything at all. Darius was mean to him, but Bartholomew didn't care. Mordecai, the other boy from his town, ganged up with the other slave-boys against Bartholomew, but Bartholomew didn't care. *Nothing matters anymore*, he just kept thinking. Nothing could make things any worse.

But then, things got worse.

It happened while he was emptying the chamber pots one morning. The master's pot was more full than usual on this day, and Bartholomew had to scrunch up his nose extra hard to keep out the smell. But with his mind still numb from the news about his parents, he didn't realize he had entered the master's bedroom too early. As he carefully carried the pot across the colorful tile floor, the master suddenly entered from his closet.

"Boy!" he yelled out, angered at seeing the slave in his room while he was still there.

The word struck Bartholomew like the crack of a whip, startling him so much that he dropped the chamber pot. The pot smashed into a thousand pieces, spreading its contents all over the sun, moon, and stars in the floor.

The master turned red and began hollering, "Hasbah! Hasbaaaaaaah!"

Hasbah came running into the room, his face as white as the marble of the master's bed. "Look what this useless boy has done!" the master screamed. "I want him whipped! I want him beaten! I want him . . ." But before he could finish his sentence, the master slipped on the wet floor and fell into his own sewage. His face went absolutely purple with rage as he screamed, "Get me out of this!"

By now several of the other slaves had run into the room, and three of them helped the master up as Bartholomew stood against the bed, crying. On his feet now, the master said in a voice that sounded like a yapping dog, "Take . . . that . . . boy . . . out . . . and cut off his hands!"

Bartholomew gasped, his throat strangled in fear. The other slaves froze where they were, staring at the master. Even Hasbah looked shocked, and after a moment he said, "But, Master, if we cut off the boy's hands, he won't be able to do his chores."

The master considered this, then said, "Very well." Bartholomew breathed a sigh of relief, as did the other slaves. But then the master said, "Have him finish his chores. And then at sunset, *cut . . . off . . . his . . . hands!*" The master glared at Bartholomew as he said this, and once again Hasbah tried to argue the point.

"Hasbah!" the master barked, and Hasbah knew the discussion was over.

"Yes, Master," he said, hanging his head. Then he led Bartholomew out by the arm, telling three of the other slaves to clean up the mess.

"Hasbah, please!" Bartholomew whispered, desperate.

"Quiet, boy," the older slave said. "Your fate is sealed."

Bartholomew went back to work, the stench of the master's chamber pot on his clothes, and the stench of fear in his heart. His head buzzed like a hornets' nest. He kept looking at his hands, not believing that tonight they would no longer be on the ends of his arms. But then he saw the slave Belka sharpening an axe, and watched out of the corner of his eye as Belka practiced swinging it onto a stump, and knew that the master's orders would be carried out no matter what. The fear inside him upset him so much that he vomited, right there in the courtyard, behind a sticker bush.

All the other slaves kept looking at Bartholomew all day. A few pairs of eyes showed sympathy, but most only curiosity. Mordecai, the other boy from Taricheae, sneered at him and laughed. *Maybe the Messiah will save me at just the right moment*, Bartholomew kept thinking.

Bartholomew watched the sun all day, willing it to stop moving. But it didn't. And just as it hid itself behind the west side of the house, Hasbah entered the courtyard. "Bartholomew!" he called. "It is time."

Slowly, with all the other slaves watching—with Hasbah waiting, hands on his hips— Bartholomew stood shakily to his feet. Then he noticed the master, watching from a window overlooking the courtyard. Bartholomew took a step toward Hasbah, then another, using all his will to make him do this thing which was the last of all the things in the world he wanted to do.

But then, in a moment that he had not planned, Bartholomew did a thing that made no sense at all. With all the other slaves watching and with Hasbah standing there waiting and with the master glaring at him from the window, Bartholomew turned and ran.

Through the door into the main house and down the cold hallway he ran, his sandals slapping loudly on the stone floor. Then out through the open front door and down the street. He pushed his way through the crowds of people, dodging horse-pulled carts, leaping over beggars with their pots of coins. Fighting for his life, terrified of the demons that chased him, Bartholomew put extra force into his running. For in the distance, back toward the house of the skunk-faced man, he could already hear the cries, "Runaway! Catch the runaway slave!"

Bartholomew turned a corner, up a street that was made mostly of stairs. Past stalls of cheese and fish and vegetables, past a dealer in copper and three selling wine. "Runaway!" the cries grew louder, and the people around him started to notice. He darted to his left, down a narrow alley that smelled like the chamber pots he emptied every day. A turn to the right, following a street that curved past a building with pillars. Then Bartholomew felt like he'd been struck by lightning as he realized he'd just gone in a circle and was back by the three wine sellers.

He could see Hasbah now, at the bottom of the stairway street, still yelling, "Runaway!" and, "Catch that boy!" He started to run uphill again, then noticed two Roman soldiers who had just heard Hasbah's cries. Slowly at first, then with gaining interest, the soldiers rose from the table where they sat drinking wine and stared at the boy. Suddenly they understood and started down the hill toward Bartholomew, running in great strides that seemed longer than that of a horse. Hasbah was closing in from below, the soldiers were running from above, so Bartholomew ran the only direction he could, through an archway to his right.

Bartholomew screamed. He had run straight into the marketplace where he'd first been sold and straight to the pit of snakes. Teetering on the edge, his toes wiggling in midair and his arms waving to keep his balance, it seemed to Bartholomew that the snakes were looking up at him, their fangs dripping with poison. He took a step back and regained his balance. But he was shivering like a freezing kitten, both because of the close call he'd just had and because he knew he really would end up in the pit if he were caught.

The shock of the incident forced Bartholomew's mind to start thinking again, and he saw that his only way out was across the courtyard and out the door on the other side. If he could make it to some side street perhaps he could . . .

Two more Roman soldiers came running in through that very door. Breathless, they searched the crowd, then spied their prey. Bartholomew ran to his right, pushing through the crowd, looking for any door or hole or friendly face that might save him.

"Runaway!" one of the Romans bellowed, and his voice bounced back and forth off the walls. All the women screamed. All in the courtyard stopped what they were doing and looked around frantically, finally spotting Bartholomew. Bartholomew saw the other two Roman soldiers enter through the archway, with Hasbah directly behind them. He backed against the courtyard wall, tears blurring his eyes. He felt as if the snakes from the pit now filled his stomach. "Jehovah, save me!" he whispered in a trembling voice.

Slowly the four Romans and Hasbah began to converge on Bartholomew, herding him as shepherds herd their sheep. The crowd parted, making way for the men who would take care of this most dangerous criminal. Eyes locked on Bartholomew like a hawk's eyes on a rat, the soldiers backed him into a corner. One pulled a net from his belt, another a rope with a noose on the end. Like hungry dogs drooling over a crippled lamb, they marched toward Bartholomew until there was nowhere for him to run.

And it was exactly at that moment that a cry like that of an angry eagle went up from somewhere in the crowd. With three flips and a cartwheel, a man dressed in the hat and tunic of a fool shot past the Roman guards and landed feet first and hands-on-hips between them and Bartholomew.

"And what, may I ask," said the fool, "do you fine fellows want with my son?"

Storms come and storms go. Tragedies strike that seem to take away all reason to live. Evil stalks us every day, waiting for its chance to wring all the joy out of our lives.

But at just that moment when things seem their worst, and it seems that nothing could possibly save us, our Father in heaven steps in.

"Because he loves me," says the LORD, "I will rescue him; I will protect him, for he acknowledges my name. He will call upon me, and I will answer him; I will be with him in trouble."   PSALM 91:14–15

That's the message of Christmas. That's the hope of Advent. That's the joy we can find in Jesus.

Fool's Gold

Light the first violet candle.

At the words of the fool the Roman soldiers stopped, looking at each other in confusion. Who was this fool? Father of a slave-boy? Or liar and thief?

Before they had a chance to think about this, the fool began bouncing back and forth between the four Romans and Hasbah. "Who do you think you are?" he squealed. "Trying to steal a boy from his father! Why, without my son, who would help me fly my kites? Who would take my feet on a walk when I'm too tired to go myself? Who would think my thoughts for me when my head won't think for itself?" Then the fool did a cartwheel over to Bartholomew, landing directly in front of him. "How dare you take my poor son!" He turned to the boy and whispered, "What's your name, boy?"

Bartholomew was almost too shocked to understand, but all his own tradings and dealings had taught him to think in a flash. "Bar . . . Bartholomew," he whispered.

"How dare you take my poor son Bartholomew," the fool continued in a loud voice. "You have no right! You have no law! You have no chicken!"

This last statement confused the soldiers even more, but the crowd in the market now laughed at the fool. Someone yelled at the soldiers to let the boy go, and the crowd murmured its agreement. The Romans seemed to hesitate, but just then one of the other slaves came running up and handed Hasbah a sheet of parchment. Hasbah spoke up in a voice like that of a lion. "My master has legal right to this boy!" he roared, waving the parchment overhead. "This bill of sale proves the matter!"

The soldiers were obviously impressed, and one started to reach for the parchment, but the fool did two giant backward flips, snagged the parchment from the hand of Hasbah, then flipped out into the crowd, which parted like the Red Sea. He held the parchment up, turning it this way and that. "Why, this note is a fake! It was written upside down!"

One of the Romans walked over to the fool and looked at the parchment, then turned it right side up. "Oh," the fool said. "Perhaps it is I who is upside-down!"

The crowd laughed again, and the Roman read the parchment. "This says the boy belongs to Festavian," he said aloud.

"No!" the fool screamed, running in circles. "It cannot be! My poor Bartholomew is no man's slave! He was stolen, he was! Yes, that's it! He was stolen, and now I have found him."

The Roman gave an impatient look and said, "Stolen or not, the boy goes back to his master."

"No!" the fool screamed again, falling at Bartholomew's feet and hugging his legs. "You cannot have him! I shall not return to the leper colony without him!"

At the words "leper colony" the crowd gasped and started to move away. Even the Roman soldiers looked nervous and took a step backward. Only Hasbah stood his ground, a disgusted look on his face. "He's lying," he said, loud enough to fill the marketplace. "He's no leper!"

Suddenly the fool jumped to his feet, stood next to Bartholomew, and crossed his arms. "You are correct," he said as if he were giving the time of day. "But please save his fingers as they fall off, so I'll have something to remember him by."

Now many in the crowd screamed, and some started pushing their way out through the archways to escape the deadly disease. Hasbah started yelling at the soldiers to grab the slave, and the soldiers yelled that they wanted nothing to do with a leper boy. It was during all this confusion that the fool grabbed Bartholomew by the hand. "Now!" he hissed, pulling Bartholomew behind him.

Before anyone could notice, the fool pulled Bartholomew up on a cart of goat cheese, then up on top of a short wall. They ran along the top of the wall to where it joined one of the outside walls of the courtyard, right above the pit of snakes. As if he were running on gazelle legs, the fool leaped to the top of the wall, then leaned down and reached for Bartholomew. "Hurry, boy," he yelled, "or we shall both be in that pit by morning!" Bartholomew hesitated, knowing that if his hand should slip from the fool's he'd fall straight into the snakes. But the sound of soldiers running toward him forced Bartholomew to reach upward. The fool grabbed Bartholomew's hands and the boy felt himself flying through the air, the pit of snakes pulling at his still-running feet. The fool pushed the boy up and over a wall, then climbed over himself. Below they saw the soldiers running toward them, Hasbah having convinced them to give chase.

On top of a roof now, the two fugitives picked themselves up and ran. "Quickly, boy," the fool yelled. "The gates shall be sealed within moments!"

The sun had set by now, and the last of the pink sky was fading into black. The fool and Bartholomew ran from roof to roof, zigzagging their way above the town. Finally they came to a house near the edge of the city and practically dove down the hole in its roof, hitting only two or three rungs of the ladder.

"Pardon us," the fool said to the family sitting in a circle on the floor, their dinner half eaten. "Pardon us," he said again as they ran through. "We seem to have lost our way." Almost before he had finished saying this, the fool was across the room and out the door, into the cool night air. Bartholomew was right on his heels, and the two ran down the street toward the nearest city gate. Just then the blast of a horn echoed off the walls, coming from somewhere in the middle of the town. An alarm, Bartholomew knew. A warning that something was wrong. Instantly four Roman guards began closing the gate that towered over their heads. But as the heavy wooden doors began to move, the fool began screaming. "Lepers!" he yelled. "Hold the gate for lepers! Unclean! Unclean!"

At the sound of "lepers" the Romans stopped and staggered backward as fast as they could. Pulling Bartholomew by the hand, the fool ran through the gates and out into the night. They ran toward the waters of the Mediterranean Sea, then scampered across the rocky cliffs that overlooked the sand below. Suddenly Bartholomew could no longer see the fool and thought he was lost, until a hand reached up through a giant crack in the rocks and grabbed Bartholomew's foot. Bartholomew fell down into the hole, landing softly in the arms of the fool. Breathing hard, the fool carried the boy back into the deepest crevices of a cold and damp cave. There a fire smoldered, and Bartholomew felt its warmth as the fool set him down next to its embers.

"Greetings, Bartholomew," the fool said, still panting hard but bowing in formal introduction. "My name is Nathan, and you will be safe with me."

Why doesn't God prevent bad things from happening to us? Why doesn't He just reach down and stop them before they start? Or send His guardian angels to protect us?

Well, maybe He does. We'll never know how many times God has stepped in to protect us, or guide us, or prevent some evil. But sometimes He can't. It seems kind of strange, but it's His great love for us that sometimes prevents Him from helping us. He has given us a free will, to do as we please. We are not slaves to Him, He doesn't force us to follow His rules. He only offers us the joy of an abundant life if we do, and then He allows us to make our own choice.

But the price of that freedom is that He has no control over some of the storms and tragedies we face.

Nathan can't do anything to bring back Bartholomew's parents or friends or the life he knew back in Taricheae. What he *can* do is help Bartholomew find a *new* life. He can say to him words much like those Jesus said to His disciples:

Do not let your heart be troubled. Trust in God; trust also in me. JOHN 14:1

When Bartholomew was being chased by evil men, he called to Jehovah for help, and God sent Nathan. If you're struggling through difficult times this Advent, or if you face such times in the future, or if you just need a friend, remember that God is only a whisper away.

Friend or Foe?

Light the first violet candle.

The smell of roasting meat tickled Bartholomew's nose until his dreams turned to Sabbath meals and ribs of deer. Then his eyes fluttered open and he sat straight up, trying to figure out where he was. The place was cold and damp—a cave—and sunlight entered through a hole at the other end. No! Not a hole! An archway!

Suddenly Bartholomew remembered the night before, and he spun around to see the fool sitting by a fire, roasting a piece of meat on a stick. "And how is the stomach of my young friend this morning?" he asked.

Bartholomew gulped and looked at the meat. "Lonely and hurting," he replied. Nathan tested the meat with his fingers, then held it out to Bartholomew, who bit it off the end of the stick like a frog snapping up a fly. The meat was burning hot, but Bartholomew didn't care. It was the first food he'd had in a day, and the first meat in five.

As Bartholomew ate, Nathan spoke. "We must leave this place soon," he said. Then, answering the startled look on Bartholomew's face, he added, "The Romans will search every inch of Caesarea. They do not give up easily when they have been embarrassed. As soon as you've eaten your fill, we'll pack up and head back into the city."

Bartholomew gulped down the meat and gasped. "Back to the *city!*" he said. "Why would we want to do *that?*"

Nathan sighed a deep sigh. "The Romans put up guard posts just down the road above us and all through the hills, each one watching the land between himself and the next guard. We will not get through such a ring of Romans without help."

Bartholomew was glum but hungry enough to take another piece of meat. "Fear not, my small friend," Nathan said, patting the boy on the shoulder. "I have many friends in Caesarea. We will fare well."

Bartholomew finished the last of the meat, along with a piece of bread and some water, as Nathan began pulling clothes out of a leather bag. Soon he had put on a pure white tunic edged with fine stitchery. Slowly, eyes closed and lips moving silently, he slid a prayer shawl over his head. The change from the tattered clothes of the fool to the royal-looking tunic of a high priest was so great that Bartholomew thought he wouldn't have known it was Nathan had he not seen it with his own eyes.

Next it was Bartholomew's turn, and Nathan wrapped him in a tunic made of the light and colorful fabric Bartholomew had seen on so many travelers in town. "A gift from an old friend," he said, and by folding and tucking the tunic just so, he made it fit Bartholomew like a butterfly in a cocoon. Then, with the fire doused and the fool outfit packed, Nathan led the way out the arched doorway of the cave.

Bartholomew gasped. Towering overhead was the strangest building he had ever seen. It was made of brick, was only as wide as his father's boat was long, but went on for as far as Bartholomew could see. But the building wasn't solid like all the other buildings he knew. This one was full of holes—archways that soared high above Bartholomew's head. Where an arch met the ground there was a short wall, and then the next archway started. It was along the top of *this* that they had run the night before, Bartholomew realized, not some cliff of rocks. And the cave was not a cave at all, but a place where an archway was half buried in the sandy beach.

"What is *this*?" Bartholomew yelled.

Nathan clamped his hand over the boy's mouth, looked around nervously, then whispered, "It's called an aqueduct. It comes from high in the mountains and is how the Romans get water into the city."

Bartholomew was amazed, and he could have stood there staring all day, but Nathan pulled him to the corner of the nearest archway. Slowly, carefully, he peeked around the corner. Bartholomew copied his move and saw a road running by in front of them.

A steady stream of people was passing by on the road, half of them going into Caesarea, half leaving it. To his right, away from the city, Bartholomew saw a squad of Roman soldiers stopping and questioning every traveler.

Nathan took a deep breath, grabbed Bartholomew's hand, then said, "Go!" With the speed of a jackrabbit the two fugitives scurried out to the road and fell in line with the people traveling into Caesarea. Nathan looked behind them several times but was finally satisfied that their move had not been noticed.

Bartholomew looked to his right, then left toward the aqueduct that followed to the side of the road. There he saw a patrol of soldiers on horses checking each and every archway of the aqueduct. He gave a little shudder at the thought of how nearly they had come to being discovered, and he pulled himself closer to Nathan.

As they approached the gate to the great city, Nathan worked his way over to a group of Jewish priests headed the same direction. By nodding his head and listening intently to their conversation, he made it look as if both he and his boy-servant were members of this group—certainly not the outlaws the guards at the gate were watching for.

Once in town, Nathan stayed with the group of priests as long as he could, then steered Bartholomew down a narrow side street. He stopped at a wooden door below a sign that read "Tanner" and knocked quietly. The door opened a crack, then swung open quickly, revealing a woman wearing an apron over her tunic. "Nathan!" she exclaimed. "Whatever happened to you last night?"

Nathan pulled Bartholomew quickly inside and closed the door. "Forgive me, Dorcas," he said. "I had a slight delay."

"Well, no matter," the plump woman said with a wave of her hand. Then she called through a doorway in the back. "Timothy! Timothy! Nathan is here!" Turning back to Nathan she said, "Timothy was so worried about you last night that he went to see a friend of yours." She turned to the doorway and called again. "Timothy! Come quickly! And bring Cornelius!"

At the name of Cornelius, Nathan drew a sharp breath. As quick as a flash of Galilean lightning, he grabbed Bartholomew and pushed him through a small doorway behind the fireplace. Just as the little door slammed shut behind Bartholomew, he heard Nathan say loudly, "Cornelius! How good to see you!"

And as Bartholomew looked through the cracks in the door he saw the biggest Roman soldier he had ever seen.

Bartholomew has found a true man of God to be his friend. Nathan *could* have just walked away and abandoned Bartholomew. He didn't have to risk being arrested, or go out of his way to care for the boy, or help him escape the Romans.

But he did. Nathan cares more about others than about himself, just as God has commanded us to do.

When we see someone who needs help, we often say to ourselves, "What's in it for me?" or "How much of my time will this take?" or "How much is this going to cost me?" What we *should* say—what God has *told* us to say—is simply, "How can I help?"

Just about every sin is nothing more than selfishness. Sometimes we are selfish by wanting things our own way. Sometimes by taking things from others, hurting others, or lying about others. But sometimes we are selfish just because we refuse to *help* others.

Jesus said to seek first the kingdom of God (Matthew 6:33). In other words, try to think most about what God wants, instead of what *you* want. Try your best to be unselfish, just as Jesus was unselfish in all He did for you.

Bartholomew isn't out of the woods yet. But because Nathan cares more about others than he does about himself, Bartholomew now has a friend to help him through whatever lies ahead.

Toy Soldiers

Light the first two violet candles.

Bartholomew watched the Roman through the cracks in the door. He was taller than any man Bartholomew had ever seen, but not much older than his oldest brother. He wore the full uniform of a soldier, complete with double-edged sword on his hip and throwing lance in his hand, but somehow the uniform didn't seem to fit too well.

"Cornelius!" Bartholomew heard Nathan say to the Roman. "I was hoping I'd get to see you on this trip!"

"The joy is all mine," the soldier said, but Bartholomew didn't think there was much joy in his voice. "At least I hope it will be," he added.

Nathan looked at the soldier for a long moment, then said slowly, "Your life is as full of joy as you choose it to be, Cornelius."

The soldier thought about these words for a moment, then said, "We had an incident yesterday, Nathan. A runaway slave. And a man dressed as a fool who helped him escape."

There was a long pause as the two men stared at each other, with Timothy and his wife looking on. Then Nathan sat on a wooden bench at a long wooden table and said, "Come, Cornelius. Let us sit and talk awhile."

The soldier didn't move but said in a low voice, "If I were to look in your bag, Nathan, would I find your fool's costume?"

Nathan tried to laugh, but it didn't sound very real. "I always travel with my fool's cap. You know that, Cornelius!"

"Yes, I do," the tall man said, his armor clinking as he moved. "And I have to wonder, is it my friend for whom our garrison is searching?"

Nathan stared at the other man for a long time, then said in a voice that was almost a whisper, "Please, Cornelius. Sit and talk."

The soldier who was barely a man hesitated, then leaned his lance against the wall and sat across from Nathan at the table. "You have opened my eyes to many things, Nathan," he said. "You tell me there is but one God, and I think I believe you. You tell me He will send a Messiah, and it seems to make sense. But this thing you cannot tell me: You cannot tell me to turn my back on my duty and my honor. Your God would not want such a thing, I must think, or He wouldn't be much of a God."

Nathan took his time responding, and Bartholomew could see that his new friend was nervous. "Our God is indeed a God of honor," he said finally. "But sometimes a man must ask, honor toward what? Toward a law that allows one man to hate another for his own personal gain? Or should duty and honor be toward something higher? Duty to truth? Honor to the law of love?"

"The law is the law, Nathan," the soldier said, a hint of anger rising in his voice. "Without the law we would have chaos. It is not for me to say what is right and what is wrong!"

"It is for *every* man to decide that!" Nathan snapped. "Right or wrong is *not* what public opinion says it is! It is written in the love that Jehovah has placed in every heart!"

Bartholomew watched as Cornelius shook his head. "No," he said. "It is written in the laws and rules that my commanders hand to me."

Just then Bartholomew heard the footfalls of an approaching Roman patrol, marching in time up the narrow street. He saw Cornelius stand and take up his lance. "That will be my squad," he said. "I must report you to my centurion. Where is the boy?"

"Cornelius, *please*," Nathan said. "Turn me in, fine, do what you will with me. But allow the boy to have his life!"

The soldier started for the door. "We will search this place and find him," he said, with no joy in his voice but with all the determination in the world.

"Cornelius!" Nathan yelled, trying to stop the Roman. "Your own family came from a line of slaves! Can you not have pity on one small boy?"

The sound of the Roman squad was loud now, and Bartholomew could feel the floor shake with every footfall. "My family has nothing to do with this boy," Cornelius said loudly, putting his hand on the latch to the door. "And I was never a slave myself."

"You were a slave to sin until I found you!" Nathan countered. "It was the love of Jehovah that straightened your ways! Can you not show that same mercy to an orphan boy?" Cornelius said nothing and started to open the door.

"Cornelius!" Nathan screamed in desperation. "The boy's master is Festavian! You *know* what that means!"

Bartholomew saw a quick shudder pass through the Roman's body, and for the first time the soldier hesitated. The pounding feet of Cornelius's squad was right outside now, and the sound shook the house like thunder. Through the crack in the open door Bartholomew could see the red capes and bronze armor of the soldiers flashing by. Then Cornelius threw his shoulders back and opened the door to Bartholomew's death.

Sometimes it's hard for us to know what's right and what's wrong. If everyone else thinks that something's OK—especially the people we want to be friends with—then it must be right. Right?

But whether it's the Greeks and Romans using people for their own pleasure, or slavery in the early days of America, or the Holocaust of World War II, or alcohol and drug abuse today, there are some things that are simply wrong. It doesn't matter if the whole world thinks it's OK, because *wrong* is *wrong* no matter what public opinion says.

God has placed in every heart the knowledge of what's right and what's wrong. Some people are so hurt by others while growing up that they bury this knowledge deep inside them, where it gets lost in anger and bitterness and insecurity. Others hide this truth behind a wall of selfishness, so they can have fun at the expense of others.

But *true* fun—true *happiness*—comes when we can honestly pray the way David did:

> "I desire to do your will, O my God; your law is within my heart."
>
> PSALM 40:8

Cornelius is facing a terrible struggle between right and wrong and must make a hard choice. We also face such decisions every day. Which way will you choose?

Escape Plan

Light the first two violet candles.

Cornelius stopped, the door half open, but then, slowly, he closed the door again. For a long time he just stood, facing the door, hand on the latch, until the last echoes of the soldiers were past. Finally, in a voice so low that Bartholomew almost couldn't make out the words, Cornelius said, "No boy deserves to be a slave to Festavian."

Cornelius leaned his head against the door frame and didn't move. Nathan stood and went over to him, putting his arm around the young man's shoulders. "You have done a good thing here," he said, and Cornelius nodded slowly.

Then Bartholomew watched as Nathan came toward the door where he was hiding. Scrambling backward as far as he could into the closet, he winced at the sunlight from a window when Nathan opened the door.

"Come, Bartholomew," he said. "Everything will be all right now."

Bartholomew hesitated briefly, then climbed slowly out of the closet. Nathan took him by the shoulder and led him over to Cornelius. The look on the Roman's face betrayed his thoughts that, perhaps, he had made a mistake; perhaps he should yet run after his commander.

As Bartholomew walked toward the man who seemed like a giant, a man wearing the uniform of the men who had ruined his life, all the anger and hatred he had hidden in his heart started making its way to the surface. At first he gritted his teeth and just glared at the Roman. But as he got closer he began to tremble, so great was his anger. By the time Nathan pulled him close to Cornelius and introduced him, Bartholomew could hold it back no longer. Running the last few steps he began kicking the soldier on his bare leg and pounding on his breastplate of bronze.

"You murdered my *friends!*" he screamed. "You took my *mother and father!*"

Nathan was startled, and feared what reaction Bartholomew's attack might bring. But when he looked to the eyes of Cornelius he saw there not anger or disgust or resentment. He saw, rather, a tear. Slowly the tall Roman knelt down and took Bartholomew by the shoulders. Bartholomew was still crying and screaming and hitting, but the big man did not retaliate. Instead, he drew Bartholomew into his arms and hugged him close to his chest.

"There, child, quiet now," he said softly, and Bartholomew collapsed into his arms and sobbed. "I am truly sorry for your loss, Bartholomew," the soldier said. "If I could return your family to you I would gladly do so."

Nathan pulled Bartholomew away and held him in his arms. "Cry, Bartholomew," he said. "No man could face what you've been through and not cry."

And so Bartholomew did, with all the tears and anger that had built up for so many days. He cried for his town, and for the life he'd known there, and for himself, alone and hunted. But most of all he cried for his parents and his family. And as Bartholomew's sobs turned to sniffles, and his shaking turned to an occasional twitch, Nathan looked at the Roman soldier and said quietly, "Will you help us?"

The soldier looked as pained as if he had just tasted goat-head pie; then, without a word, he turned and went out the door.

"What do you think he'll do?" Timothy asked.

Nathan shook his head slowly. "I don't know. I have asked much of him. We must prepare ourselves for escape immediately."

Nathan, Timothy, and Dorcas discussed several plans for escaping from Caesarea, but none seemed too hopeful. Finally they decided it best if Dorcas took Bartholomew, and Nathan left with some priests. The Romans were looking for a man and a boy and might overlook a woman traveling with her son. Taking all the money they had for food, Dorcas went to the market and bought a tunic for herself and for Bartholomew. These were the expensive tunics of the wealthy Jews. Hopefully the Romans would more easily pass a woman of wealth than they would a poor Jewish handmaiden.

It was time to go. Nathan was dressed in his full priest's outfit, and Bartholomew in his new tunic of fine stitchery and laced edges. But though their plan was as ready as it could be, no one moved toward the door. Bartholomew was trembling on the inside, from fear now instead of grief. He could see that the adults were all nervous and didn't hold much hope that the plan would really work. The Romans were very methodical, after all, and would want to see papers that neither Nathan nor Dorcas would be carrying. Finally he asked, "Couldn't we just stay here and hide?"

"No, child," Nathan answered. "The Romans will soon start searching house-to-house, and no place will be safe. Our chances are better at getting past the guards at the gate and on the road."

"M-maybe the Messiah will come before the Romans can find us!" Bartholomew stammered.

Nathan sighed. "I believe the Messiah could come at any time," he said, "but I fear that will not help our present situation." Then with regret in his voice, Nathan said goodbye to his friends. "I will meet you tomorrow by the wells of Kordan," he said. He put his hand on Bartholomew's shoulder and added, "If I do not meet you, go to my home at Qumran and tell them I sent you."

"We will see that the boy gets there," Dorcas said, and Bartholomew thought it all sounded much too frightening. He had lost everything and now had finally made a friend, and he was about to lose him as well.

"Please don't leave me," Bartholomew cried, wrapping his arms around Nathan. Nathan patted the boy on the head. "Fear not, Bartholomew, we will meet again." Nathan pulled free from the boy and went to the door, but just as he was reaching for the door latch, it opened all by itself.

Standing there was the Roman soldier, Cornelius, with what looked to Bartholomew like the entire Roman army behind him.

What's inside all those neatly wrapped packages under the tree on Christmas morning? Does a big box hold a better present than a small one? Is the one that rattles when you shake it something better than the one that's silent? Can you tell how much you'll like the gift inside a package by the size of the bow on top or the color of the ribbon?

Sometimes it's easy to think so. Sometimes the shape or size or wrapping of a gift makes us believe that what's inside will make us happier than any other gift we could open. But sometimes, lots of times, we're wrong. Sometimes the most precious gift we can receive comes in the smallest, most unusual package of them all.

You just can't tell a gift by its wrapping.

And yet, like Bartholomew, we often think we can tell what's inside a person's heart by the "package" they're "wrapped" in—the clothes or uniform they wear, the place they live, or the way that they're different from us.

If you were a Jew in Bartholomew's time you'd be waiting for the Messiah to appear as a mighty warrior, charging out of heaven with an army of angels to wipe out all your enemies with a few swings of the sword. But the Messiah that God sent, the gift He gave us, was wrapped much differently than that. He was wrapped in swaddling clothes and lying in a manger.

You just never can tell what's inside a person by the way he or she is packaged!

Dangerous Roads

Light the first two violet candles.

Cornelius stared them all in the eye for a moment, and Bartholomew could see nothing but red capes and bronze shields in the street behind him.

"We are here to search this house for a runaway slave!" Cornelius roared in a voice that rattled Bartholomew's bones. Then he noticed that Cornelius had a funny look on his face. He seemed to be trying to signal them. His eyes open wide, Cornelius kept looking from Nathan to the far side of the room and back again.

"All here, give heed!" Cornelius bellowed as he continued to move his eyes, "and make way for the army of the Emperor!"

Suddenly Nathan seemed to understand what Cornelius was saying. Moving slowly, with Cornelius still blocking the view of the other soldiers, Nathan stepped backward toward the fireplace. As he passed Bartholomew he tugged on the boy's elbow, then led him to the corner. Behind the door now, where the soldiers on the street couldn't see, Bartholomew watched as Cornelius entered the little house and slammed the door behind him.

Cornelius quickly picked up a chair that was close by. "Dorcas!" he hissed. "Scream loudly!" Dorcas looked too shocked to understand. But then the boy-soldier threw the chair against the wall and, without any more prompting at all, Dorcas let out a scream that made the hairs on Bartholomew's neck stand straight up.

Cornelius started throwing other things now, including a large urn which he smashed against the fireplace. Between Dorcas's screams, Bartholomew could hear other screams and the sounds of the other houses nearby being ransacked. And suddenly, he understood.

Cornelius hurried to Nathan's side and whispered. "The engineers are shutting down the aqueduct in forty minutes," he said in a rush. "It will be closed for one hour for repairs at Kidrah. If you go quickly you can escape past the checkpoints before the waters return."

With that the Roman turned to leave, but Nathan stopped him. "Thank you, my friend," he said. "May Jehovah richly reward you for your kindness."

The young soldier paused, struggling with the conflict inside him. "If this Jehovah of yours is really as you say," he said finally, "then pray that I will meet Him properly some day."

"That I will," Nathan answered. "That I will indeed pray."

His red robes billowing in the quickness of his move, Cornelius threw one last chair. Then, with Dorcas crying loudly in the background, he turned and left the house of Timothy.

Bartholomew sucked in his breath and waited. Outside he heard Cornelius yell, "All clear, centurion!" A minute later he heard the squad of soldiers move away down the street, and, as one, all in the house let out a sigh of relief.

"Jehovah be praised!" Nathan muttered as he wiped the sweat from his forehead.

A new and more hopeful escape route now open to them, the four friends quickly devised a new plan. They waited for the sun to move half a mark across the sky, then set their plan in motion. Nathan left first, holding his prayer box in front of him and chanting softly to himself, a shawl over his head. Then Dorcas loaded Bartholomew high with baskets of cloth and bundles of household goods, and they left in a different direction. Last of all, Timothy exited, to watch from afar and lend assistance in case of trouble.

As soon as they were out in the street, Dorcas began playing the part of a rich and finicky Jewish woman. Moving slowly, she'd look over the wares of each vendor, turning her nose up at most everything, showing interest in only a few things, buying nothing because she had no more money to spend. A few times a friend or two would recognize Dorcas and start to say something, but a raised eyebrow was enough to silence them. *I guess when you live among the Romans*, Bartholomew thought, *you learn to speak without words.*

The boy and his "mother" worked their way toward the south end of Caesarea, where the aqueduct entered the city, filling the cisterns with water. A public bath was nearby, and that was where they were to meet Nathan. They were about halfway to the baths when

Bartholomew suddenly gasped and hid behind Dorcas. "What is it, boy?" she whispered without turning around.

"Hasbah!" Bartholomew said. "My taskmaster!"

Dorcas looked around and spotted a tall slave leading three other slaves, all searching every face on every boy in the market. There were no side streets to turn into and nowhere to hide. Hasbah was getting closer, and Dorcas knew they had only seconds to act. "We cannot turn back," she whispered. "They would surely see us leaving." She thought for a moment, then said, "Bartholomew, drop the baskets!"

"What?!"

"Drop the baskets you carry!"

Bartholomew could not understand at all why Dorcas would want him to do such a thing, especially when it would make a commotion Hasbah was sure to see, but having been taught to mind his elders and with his old taskmaster just a few yards away, Bartholomew knew not to argue. He dropped the baskets.

"Why, you foolish boy!" Dorcas screamed. Before Bartholomew realized what was happening, Dorcas had grabbed him by the neck of his tunic and turned him over her knee. Yelling with every slap of her hand, she began spanking Bartholomew as if he had just lost the family cow. "You stupid, foolish boy!" she shrieked. "I'll teach you to be so careless!"

That's funny, Bartholomew thought, *the spanking doesn't hurt at all*. Hanging over Dorcas's knee, all he could see was the stone pavement of the market. He could *feel* Dorcas hitting him, but she wasn't hurting him at—

Suddenly Bartholomew realized. With a great wail he began to cry as if he were receiving the whipping of his life. "Please, Mother!" he squealed. Many of the other shoppers laughed now, pleased that an insolent boy was being disciplined.

"This is the third time this week you've dropped my shopping," Dorcas was screaming. "Just wait till your father hears about this!"

Bartholomew's cries got louder, and the crowd seemed to be pleased. Hasbah stood watching, a suspicion gnawing at the back of his mind. The boy was dressed in rich clothes, but he was about the right size. If he could just get a look at his face . . .

Just then Timothy appeared from the shadows, looking bewildered. With a glance of her eyes, Dorcas pointed out the problem to Timothy, and he went and stood next to Hasbah, arms folded, shaking his head. "That poor boy," he said. "She beats him in public like that two or three times a week."

Hasbah just snorted. "A much better fate than the one that awaits the boy *I'm* searching for!" he said.

"Oh, and who is that?" Timothy asked innocently.

"A runaway slave. A boy about that size," Hasbah said, pointing to Bartholomew. "But one not so spoiled."

"May Jehovah grant you a fruitful search," Timothy said with a bow, silently asking Jehovah to do just the opposite. Hasbah snorted again, then continued on down the market, searching every face.

Seeing that the taskmaster had moved on, Dorcas ended her punishment and set Bartholomew on his feet. Moving to block Hasbah's view of the boy in case he looked back, she once again piled Bartholomew high with baskets, hiding his face. With a nod to Timothy, she took her "son" by the arm and continued up the market.

A short while later they turned a corner and saw the public baths. Bartholomew's heart began to race, and he wished he had a bucket of water to drink because his mouth was so dry he couldn't even swallow. With Dorcas leading, they strolled through the open square in front of the baths. When she was sure no one was looking, they slipped down the alley. At the back was a stone staircase that led up to a channel, which carried the water from the aqueduct to the bathhouse building. Waiting on the staircase was Nathan of Qumran.

"Greetings, friends," he said. "I was starting to think you might not join me."

"A slight delay," Dorcas said, quickly setting Bartholomew's baskets on the ground. "I had to stop and spank the boy," she said. Nathan was shocked at this and obviously didn't understand. Bartholomew just laughed, his first laugh since the Romans burned his town.

"I'll hear of this later," Nathan said. "For now, we must go quickly. The waters have already stopped flowing, and we have very little time." Just then Timothy entered the alleyway, and Nathan said to both of them, "A thousand thanks for your help. If I am not able to reward you, may Jehovah do so in my place."

Timothy and Dorcas smiled and nodded, then Timothy said, "Go now. We will watch this alley for a time."

With that, Nathan took Bartholomew by the hand and climbed the narrow stairway. They turned a corner, then climbed some more, finally ending up on top, where a channel had been built into the roof. The channel was about as wide as a cart and made of brick. It was still wet from the water that had been flowing through it only minutes before. Nathan jumped down into the channel, which came up to his waist, then lifted Bartholomew down. The sun was straight overhead now, and it turned the water on the bricks to steam.

Moving quickly, the two fugitives climbed the gentle slope of the channel until they got to the point where it joined the larger aqueduct. Bars of rusty iron covered the hole where water would leave the aqueduct and enter the channel, so Nathan lifted Bartholomew up on top of the larger waterway, then climbed up himself.

The aqueduct itself was so wide that two horses could have raced up it side by side, and deep enough that Nathan could stand up straight and still not look over the edge. Nathan lowered Bartholomew into the empty canal, then jumped down himself. Bartholomew looked along the long course of the aqueduct and realized that if the water suddenly came around the corner, there would be no time to jump out of its way.

Moving quickly once again, Nathan led the way up the slight incline of the aqueduct. They passed two buildings that were taller than the waterway, and Bartholomew hoped that no one would look out a window and see them. Then they reached the city wall. More iron bars blocked the aqueduct where it ran through the wall. But Nathan was ready for this, and pulled out a tool that looked like a funny sort of fish hook. Using the leverage of the tool, Nathan soon had two of the bars parted enough that he could squeeze through. Bartholomew followed as easily as a cat sneaking through a fence. But just as they were entering the short tunnel where the aqueduct passed through the wall, Bartholomew heard the pounding feet of a Roman army squad. The sound stopped just below the aqueduct, and Bartholomew could hear the commander giving orders.

"You three!" he bellowed, "Search the buildings of the temple. You two!" he continued, "Search the bathhouse. And you!" he barked, "Guard the aqueduct at the wall. With the water stopped, they may try to escape that way!" Together the several soldiers responded, "As you command!"

Nathan had heard the soldiers as well and looked quickly around for a place to hide. There was none. The shadows of the tunnel offered the only hope, and Nathan and Bartholomew hugged the side, having nowhere else to go. They heard the quick steps of the soldier climbing the stairway, then saw his shadow on the aqueduct floor as he towered over them. With a single leap that Bartholomew thought should surely break his legs, the soldier jumped into the aqueduct, landing solidly on his feet. Bartholomew felt Nathan tense, and this only made him more frightened. The soldier had his back to them and was looking back toward town. Bartholomew looked at the sharp point of the soldier's lance and the double-edged sword that hung on his hip.

Trapped by the sides of the aqueduct, nowhere to hide and nowhere to run, Bartholomew felt like a fish caught in a net. And he knew very well what happened to fish when they were caught. He could almost feel himself being cleaned and gutted as the soldier drew his sword—and turned toward him.

Have you ever felt as if you were trapped in a bad situation? Have you ever felt as if you had no choice, no escape, nowhere to run? Have you ever felt helpless, or alone, or afraid?

In times like those, when it seems impossible that anything could help you, or save you, or comfort you, remember the secret God shared with us on Christmas day. Remember that there is a "name that is above every name" (Philippians 2:9) you can call on, a friend who is ready to help, a God who is standing by to rescue.

Remember that name. And when all else fails, and nothing else can help, call on that name . . . Jesus!

Soldier's Surprise

Light the first two violet candles.

The soldier started to turn, and Bartholomew thought that surely running was better than sitting and being caught. He was just about to jump up when the soldier turned fully in their direction and saw them.

And then he smiled.

"I was wondering if I'd find you here," Cornelius whispered.

Nathan collapsed against the wall of the tunnel, and Bartholomew just about wet his tunic. "I'm glad to see it is you, my friend," Nathan gasped. "May Jehovah bless you with a long and prosperous life!"

Cornelius considered this for a moment. "I'm still not sure about your God," he said finally, "but I'm beginning to think He is more powerful than my commanders. I didn't ask to be assigned to search the house of Timothy. Nor did I ask to be sent to the top of this aqueduct. It would seem your God is watching out for you."

"As He has for many years, Cornelius."

The boy-soldier sighed a deep sigh. "Perhaps we can speak of this again someday," he said.

"As soon as it is safe for me to return here," Nathan answered.

Cornelius smiled again, which looked very strange for a Roman soldier, Bartholomew thought. "Go now," he said. "And may the gods . . . that is, may Jehovah be with you."

Nathan waved and turned, and Bartholomew followed, but then the boy stopped and turned back. He stared at the Roman for several seconds, then, in a loud whisper, said simply, "Thank you."

Cornelius nodded, then Bartholomew turned away again and followed Nathan quickly up the aqueduct. The canal was like a road for him, a road that led away from Caesarea and the horrors of slavery and the life he once knew. Where that road would lead he did not know, but as he followed Nathan up the sun-warmed bricks, he knew that Jehovah was, indeed, watching over him.

Nathan and Bartholomew hurried up the canal formed by the aqueduct. The walls were too high for Bartholomew to see over, but he knew they were running parallel to the road and about twenty feet above it. They had to get far beyond the last checkpoint on the road, he knew, before the Roman engineers finished their repairs up in the mountains and once again released the water.

"Quickly, boy," Nathan panted. "We have far to go."

Bartholomew was pretty sure he could run farther and longer than his older friend, and he wasn't even yet breathing hard, but he decided not to say anything. He had learned long ago to honor his elders in all things. That is, unless they planned to chop off his hands!

As he ran, thoughts of Cornelius filled Bartholomew's head. He was all confused now, and didn't know what to think. He had just figured that all Romans were evil demons in the sight of God, but then this particular Roman—and a soldier no less—was friendly and even defied his own commanders to help Bartholomew. *Were the Romans evil people or not?* he wondered.

The sun had not traveled very far across the sky before Nathan slowed to a stop and bent over, panting hard. "We'll . . . we'll take a rest for a moment," he said. Bartholomew still wasn't breathing hard, but he said nothing. When he had caught his breath, Nathan said, "Let me lift you up to see where we are."

Bartholomew wasn't so sure he wanted to take a chance on being seen, but again he said nothing. Nathan lifted the boy to where he could just peek over the top edge of the aqueduct. Below them he saw the road, and, just to his right about twenty paces, a Roman checkpoint. The guards were stopping all the people coming out of Caesarea and searching all the carts. One soldier stopped for a moment to wipe the sweat from his forehead and looked straight at Bartholomew. The boy ducked but was none too sure that he hadn't been seen. Without warning he dropped to the floor of the canal, knocking Nathan down.

"Romans!" he gasped. "A checkpoint."

Nathan looked glum but stood and gathered his bags. "We'd better hurry," he whispered. Stepping as softly as they could, the two continued on up the aqueduct, leaving the checkpoint behind. When they had traveled what Bartholomew thought must be halfway across Palestine, Nathan stopped.

"What is it?" Bartholomew asked.

Nathan held up his hand for silence. Finally he said, "That roaring sound."

Bartholomew nodded. "Isn't it just a waterfall?"

Nathan looked at the boy with a crooked smile. "There *are* no waterfalls near here. They must have opened the aqueduct."

With wide open eyes Bartholomew yelled, "What'll we do?" Nathan hoped there were no Romans below to hear.

"It is time to leave our private road," he answered. And with that, he lifted Bartholomew to the wall of the canal on the opposite side from the road. "What do you see?" he asked.

Bartholomew studied the terrain, then said, "The road is empty. But there's an awful lot of water coming down the aqueduct."

The way Bartholomew said it, so casually, made it sound like nothing important. But Nathan knew he had only seconds to act. With one eye on the corner ahead, he leaped for the top of the wall, just barely grabbing it with his fingertips. At that moment a wave of water came racing around the corner. Nathan pulled himself up far enough to grab the far edge of the wall, but then the water struck, sweeping his body along with it. Bartholomew grabbed his friend by the wrist and pulled with all his might. If he slipped, the water would carry Nathan back to the center of Caesarea before he even had time to take a breath.

Nathan dug his fingers into a crack between the bricks, then got one foot up on the wall and pulled himself up. He lay there wheezing, "Well, . . . at least . . . I've had . . . my bath . . . for the day!"

Bartholomew sat staring at him for a moment, soaking wet, heart racing, then started to laugh. Just a little at first, but then so hard that Nathan feared he would fall in the water.

A short time later the two travelers found a place where the sand reached almost to the top of the wall and jumped down. On the road now, they began the long journey to . . .

Suddenly Bartholomew realized he had no idea where they were going, so he asked.

"To Qumran, my home," Nathan said.

"Where is that?" Bartholomew asked.

"On the far north end of the Sea of Death."

Bartholomew scrunched up his nose. He loved the waters of the Sea of Galilee, full of fish and life and boats, and would rather be near a sea than anywhere else in the world. But this he did not understand. "Why would you want to live *there*?" he asked.

Nathan sighed. "I guess it just seemed like the right place to build a community," he answered. And then he went on to explain that Qumran was the old building site of the Essenes, the religious group Nathan belonged to. It had been destroyed by an earthquake many years before and had lain in ruins since. "When we decided to rebuild our community, it seemed natural to rebuild our village as well," Nathan concluded.

"But why in the middle of the desert? Why not in Galilee, where it's green and there are trees and fish and water that is not dead?"

Nathan sighed again. "Perhaps to remind us that we are all in a spiritual desert of death until the Messiah comes."

Bartholomew thought about this. He knew of the Messiah, of course—his father had taught him many such things. And since he had turned ten, Bartholomew had been attending reading classes with the rabbi. But what the Messiah had to do with the desert, he did not understand.

"Think like this," Nathan said. "In a desert, no matter what good thing you plant, it will whither and die because there is no water. If our lives are a desert, barren of any devotion to God, then any good thing we try to do will waste away, because we don't have the living water of Jehovah's love. And until we have the fertile field of the Messiah, none of us will truly understand that love."

They started into the hills of Judea, climbing steadily higher, as Bartholomew thought of these things. "So the Romans are deserts, and we Jews are green fields," he said after a long think. "Does that mean Cornelius cannot know Jehovah?"

Nathan shook his head. "Whether a man's life is a desert or not has nothing to do with being a Jew or a Roman. I know many Jews whose lives are barren and empty, and a few

Romans like Cornelius who thirst for the water of truth. I do not believe the Messiah will care so much about a man's heritage as He will his heart."

They were just cresting a hill, one of hundreds of hills of the mountain desert, and Bartholomew asked, "When the Messiah comes, will He kill *all* the Romans or just the bad ones?"

Nathan started to answer, then suddenly stopped walking, grabbed Bartholomew under his arms, and dove for the side of the road, behind a huge boulder. Bartholomew yelped in shock, and Nathan covered his mouth. "Quiet, my friend," he said. "A caravan approaches. Friend or foe, I do not know."

Slowly, Nathan lifted himself to where he could look over the top of the boulder. Being ten years old and curious, Bartholomew couldn't stand not seeing for himself, so he, too, slowly stood until just his eyes showed above the rock. What he saw made his heart sing. This was a Jewish caravan: no Romans, no soldiers. Surely they would be safe with such a strong and mighty band.

But then Bartholomew looked at Nathan, and he saw Nathan's eyes grow wide in fear. Grabbing Bartholomew by the neck, Nathan dropped behind the rock once again. With fear in his voice and fright on his face, he whispered just three words that almost made Bartholomew want to run back to Caesarea.

"Decha of Megiddo!" Nathan whispered. And suddenly Bartholomew understood about spiritual deserts.

When the woman at the well asked Jesus what kind of water he could provide—water that was better than that of her ancestors who had dug the well—he answered:

> "Everyone who drinks this water will be thirsty again, but whoever drinks the water I give him will never thirst. Indeed, the water I give him will become in him a spring of water welling up to eternal life."   JOHN 4:13–14

So what is this "water" that Jesus offers us? Obviously it's not the kind that would irrigate a desert and grow food, but it does seem to be symbolic of something that will irrigate the desert of our hearts. What could such a thing be? What could so nourish our soul that it needs nothing else to sustain it? Simply this: the unconditional love of God.

All of us spend our lives hoping people will love us. It's a built-in need we have, just like our need for food and water. God loved us from the beginning, but then we turned our backs on Him, which left a big hole inside us. We try to fill that hole by being important to our friends, or with the praise of our parents, or by being the center of attention, by having a special friend, by making ourselves powerful, or in a thousand other ways. But all those feeble efforts leave our hearts spiritual deserts, because nothing can ever adequately fill that God-sized hole inside us.

But if we can accept the Living Water that Jesus spoke of, if we can accept that we are loved completely because God loves us, if we can accept the fact that it doesn't matter what anyone but God thinks of us, then and only then will the deserts of our souls spring to life!

Jericho

Light the first two violet candles.

Did they see us?" Bartholomew asked, hugging the boulder as if it could protect him from all bad things.

"I do not think so," Nathan answered, but Bartholomew wasn't so sure. He'd heard tales of Decha of Megiddo, one of which was that he had four pairs of eyes and knew everything that happened within a day's ride of himself.

Bartholomew scrunched down even lower as the sound of the caravan drew closer. If a scout or a stray child happened to leave the road and come around the rock, they would surely see the two hidden travelers and raise an alarm. Bartholomew decided he'd rather be back at the skunk man's house than in the camp of Decha of Megiddo.

Moments later the caravan was just on the other side of the rock. Bartholomew could hear every footstep of every beast and person and could smell their smells as well. The dust in the air carried with it the stench of camel fur and donkey dung, of unwashed pots and a hundred unwashed people. The smell made Bartholomew's stomach churn, while the noise battered his ears. He held his nose with one hand and plugged one ear with the other.

Bartholomew could see the animals and people as they passed beyond his hiding place and followed the road around a hill below. At the front of the line was a man wearing a black cape that looked big enough to make a tent, but was just the right size for the man who wore it. Every look and move of the man seemed to say, "Evil!" and Bartholomew decided this had to be Decha himself. He knew just by looking at the man that you could never escape if Decha got a hold of you.

The ground trembled with the passing of the caravan, and Bartholomew was sure the train of people and animals would never end. But then, finally, the last person waddled by—a fat old woman with black teeth—and the long line of the caravan continued down the hill and around a corner. Nathan waited several minutes to be sure there were no stragglers, then stood up and brushed himself off. As Bartholomew did the same, Nathan stared quizzically in the direction the caravan had gone.

"I wonder what Decha is doing down here," he mumbled under his breath. Bartholomew had many times heard the stories of Decha, how he raided and stole and tortured and killed. He came from the town of Megiddo, at the north end of Bartholomew's province of Galilee, but until this day Bartholomew had never seen him. Decha seemed to stay away from the bigger towns, only terrorizing small, defenseless villages.

"Well, now," Nathan said, "that was an adventure I do not care to repeat!" Then, turning to Bartholomew, he added, "Shall we continue our journey?"

Bartholomew thought that any distance they could put between them and Decha would be a good thing, so he nodded and picked up his bag.

A few hours later, with the dust of the road filling his throat and the heat of the sun drying him out like a raisin, Bartholomew asked, "Nathan, how much farther to Qumran?"

"About a day," was Nathan's reply.

Bartholomew's heart fell. This road was certainly easier than the one he'd been forced to tread to Caesarea, but except for that most unpleasant trip, he had never before been outside his town of Taricheae. All this walking was much too much work, he decided.

"But fear not," Nathan added. "We shall soon find Jericho, where we will spend the night with a friend."

Now Bartholomew's heart leapt with joy. He had heard of Jericho, of course, and his father and two oldest brothers had even gone there once, but he had never dreamed he would get to see the great city himself.

As they walked, Bartholomew got around to asking the question that had been bothering him all day. "Nathan," he said, "*will* the Messiah kill Cornelius when He comes?"

"The Messiah will kill *no one* when He comes!"

"Yes, He will! He will kill all those donkey Romans and give us back our land!"

"No, Bartholomew, I'm afraid you are mistaken. It is true that many Jews believe that is why the Messiah is coming. But in truth, if you read the Scriptures, you will find that He is coming to show us God's *love*, not His *anger*."

Bartholomew squirmed as he walked, his body acting out the conflict in his mind. "But that's not what everyone always told *me*," he said. "Everyone says the Messiah will come to kill the Romans!"

"And what does the Torah say?" Nathan asked quietly.

"I . . . I don't know," Bartholomew answered. "I've only heard stories about Abraham and Noah and such."

"Which is why your father was teaching you to read," Nathan said, "so that you can read the Torah for yourself and there find its truths."

Bartholomew thought about this as he walked. He was starting to miss his father greatly again. But then he looked up and started to feel as if perhaps life could continue on after all. For out of the desert, and next to a river that Bartholomew knew to be the Jordan, rose a city that to weary eyes looked as if it were made of gold. More objective eyes might have seen that the town was built of white mortar and stone, and that it was the glow of the setting sun that turned it to gold, but Bartholomew had no desire to be objective. It was a city almost as great as Caesarea itself, but better because this was a Jewish city, not a Roman one.

Bartholomew's eyes opened wide as he and Nathan entered the great trading port. The same traveling merchants he had seen in Caesarea seemed to be here, dressed in their colorful robes and turbans, and driving exotic animals. But there were no Romans among Jericho's citizens, and only a few soldiers to keep the peace. Bartholomew hoped that word of his escape had not traveled this far.

Nathan walked on past the stalls, where vendors of jewelry and pottery and strange-looking foods sold their wares, then down a side street past an inn and a stable, to a large wooden door, set in a wall, with no markings on it at all. Nathan knocked, and a moment later the door was opened by a large man wearing a white tunic that made him look like a Roman.

"Nathan!" the man cried with a hug and a smile. "My eyes expect a seller and instead see a friend!"

"And you are a sight that lightens the heart as well, my friend!" Nathan responded. Turning to the boy beside him he said, "Bartholomew, this is my good friend and troublemaker, Silas of Joppa. Silas, this is my new friend and companion Bartholomew, a slave-orphan, courtesy of the Romans."

A cloud covered Silas's face and he knelt his rather large bulk down to the boy. "My heart sobs with you at your loss," he said softly. "May my friendship help to fill the emptiness you feel."

Without even thinking, Bartholomew hugged the man who moments before had been a stranger.

He felt that, perhaps, his heart was indeed a little less empty.

Silas stood and led the two travelers into his house, which Bartholomew thought looked as rich as the skunk man's but much more friendly. "You'll first want a bath, no doubt," Silas said to Nathan.

"It *would* ease my soul a bit," Nathan replied, and at that two servants were called to take Nathan and Bartholomew to a room with a large pool. As the setting sun shone on them through an archway, they soaked in the cool water. The servants brought new, fresh tunics, and then they joined Silas at a table set with a great feast such as Bartholomew had seen at the skunk man's house. Only *this* time *he* got to sit down at the table.

But then he was troubled. Looking at the servants he whispered, "Are these men slaves?"

Nathan smiled and whispered back, "No, my young friend. They are employees, well paid to serve us."

With that, Bartholomew grinned and dove into the platters of food.

"So what adventures did your latest journey bring?" Silas asked of Nathan, as Bartholomew munched on the biggest duck leg he had ever seen.

"Oh, nothing out of the ordinary," Nathan said with a wink at Bartholomew. "I traveled to Caesarea to talk more with Cornelius." Silas nodded at this as he ate, obviously knowing about the young Roman soldier. "While I was there I happened on Bartholomew. He was attempting to convince some Romans that he didn't really care to have his hands chopped off."

Silas stopped eating and looked at Nathan in disgust. "Festavian?" he asked, referring to Bartholomew's former master. Nathan nodded, and Silas snorted and said, "Someone should take that skunk out and chop off *his* hands! Or worse!"

Bartholomew paused in the middle of chewing. Silas had used the exact word for Festavian that he himself used! He liked this new friend.

But Nathan half smiled and half frowned. "Now, Silas," he said, "revenge is Jehovah's to hold, not for us to order."

"Yes, yes, I know," Silas answered, "but sometimes a man is so evil that Jehovah needs a little help!"

Nathan kept looking at the wing he was chewing on as he said, "You mean a man such as Decha of Megiddo?"

Silas stopped cold and stared. "Did you see him?" he gasped.

Nathan nodded. "Just this morning. His caravan traveled south, toward Jerusalem."

Silas turned several shades of purple and a couple of red before he was able to sputter the words, "If the Messiah doesn't come soon to rid us of these demons, I swear I shall take a sword to them myself!"

Nathan sighed a deep sigh. "You know, my friend, that the Messiah is not coming to kill our enemies for us."

Silas took an angry bite out of the other duck leg. "Yes, I know," he said sadly, "but he *should!*"

"Perhaps," was all Nathan said. But Bartholomew could see thoughts to the contrary behind Nathan's eyes.

With dinner over, Silas and Nathan talked awhile, then Silas announced it was time for sleep and led them all up some stairs, past torch-lit columns, and down a hallway. There he pointed out a room for Bartholomew and one for Nathan. Nathan must have seen the distress on Bartholomew's face at the thought of being alone. He said, "Why don't we move Bartholomew's sleeping mat into my room?" And so that's what they did, and that's why it wasn't long before Bartholomew was lying snug on his mat, just a few feet from where Nathan lay on his. That's when Bartholomew asked, "Nathan, when will the Messiah come?"

"Soon, child," Nathan said with sleep in his voice, "Very soon."

Bartholomew was shocked at this, wondering how his friend could know such a thing. "*How* soon?" he asked through the darkness.

"Perhaps tomorrow," came the last words of Nathan for the day. "Perhaps tomorrow."

And any thought of sleep instantly left the ten-year-old's head.

When *will* the Messiah come? When will Jesus return to gather up His flock and take them to heaven with Him?

Some people say that will happen any day, certainly in our lifetimes. Others believe—and act as if—it will not happen for thousands of years. Who's right, and who's wrong?

The truth is, we simply do not know. "No one knows about that day or hour," Jesus said (Matthew 24:36). But by the signs He gave us, the time could indeed be very close.

Then again, the disciples thought the same thing. They expected Him to return soon after He ascended to heaven. I wonder if they would have acted differently had they known we'd still be waiting two thousand years later.

Bartholomew is beginning to understand that the coming of the Messiah is not some story being told that will have no impact on his life. He's beginning to understand that the prophecies are real and will change his life in dramatic ways.

It is so easy for us to think of God as some vague and distant power and to behave as if He doesn't matter at all. But the God we believe in, and the Son whose Advent we celebrate, is the only thing that truly matters in our lives. Not just because Jesus will return to earth someday, but because the Holy Spirit is already here, inside us, loving us and guiding us and comforting us.

Imagine what this world would be like if everyone lived as if Jesus were returning to earth tomorrow!

New Friends

Light the first two violet candles.

Bartholomew watched from the window in the room he and Nathan shared as the city of Jericho awoke. Below, he saw a vendor of fish wait until his neighbor, the vendor of cheese, was helping a customer. The fish seller snatched a bit of yellow cheese from behind his friend's back and popped it in his mouth. Over by the gate to the baths, two women in ragged clothes were begging for coins. In the middle of the market a man lost control of his camel, and several other men ran to help him recapture the crazed animal.

A snort and a cough from behind Bartholomew told him Nathan was waking up, but Bartholomew just kept staring out the window, fascinated by all the activity.

"Shalom, Bartholomew," Nathan said with a yawn. "What is it that brings you up with the sun?"

Bartholomew still didn't turn. "I never got to sleep," he said simply.

"No sleep! Why, last night you were as tired as a mule forced to carry the Rabbi! What kept you from your dreams?"

Bartholomew finally turned around and looked at his friend. "You did," he said. "You told me that the Messiah might come today, and then you fell asleep. I could think of nothing else all the night."

Nathan laughed. "It was mostly a joke, Bartholomew," he said. Then seeing the distressed look on the boy's face, he quickly added, "Yes, it is true. The Messiah *could* be born today. But it could also be tomorrow or next week or next month. No one knows for sure."

"Born! What do you mean, *born*?"

"Well," Nathan said with a smile, "when a baby comes out of its mother, we call it being born."

"I *know* that," Bartholomew answered impatiently, "but the Messiah is not a baby! He's . . . He's the *Messiah!*"

"Isaiah is very clear that the Messiah shall be born to a woman, just as you were."

"But how can a little baby kill the Romans?" Bartholomew asked.

"Did I not tell you, child, that the Messiah is not coming to kill but to love?"

Bartholomew was glum. "Yes, you did. But it is a most difficult thing to believe. Everyone always said—"

"Everyone, including your father?" Nathan interrupted.

Bartholomew thought back. "No," he said finally. "My father always spoke as you do. But . . . I didn't . . . listen."

Nathan smiled. "It is far more appealing for us to believe that the Messiah will come as a great warrior king, to destroy our enemies. But our greatest enemy, Bartholomew, is not the Romans." Bartholomew looked up in surprise as Nathan added quietly, "Our greatest enemy is our own hatred and selfishness."

Bartholomew thought about this for a long moment. "If the Messiah was born today, shouldn't we go out into the city and look for Him? Shouldn't we be there to honor Him?"

Nathan sighed. "It would be my greatest desire," he said. "But the Messiah will not be born in Jericho. This great event will happen in the City of David, in Bethlehem."

Bartholomew looked disappointed. "I was hoping to find Him out there," he said, turning back to the window.

"This cannot be," Nathan said.

Bartholomew slowly nodded his head in understanding, then asked, "May I go out into the market before breakfast?"

Nathan hesitated. "Very well. But stay close to the house of Silas, and keep away from any Romans you see!"

With a grin the size of a melon, Bartholomew was down the hall and past the columns, where he saw Silas silently praying in a small alcove that held what looked like a Torah. Bartholomew moved quietly around the pool in the center of the room and out the front door. In the market-place now, he looked this way and that, overwhelmed by all the people. *So many new friends to make*, he thought. *How will I ever meet them all?* He decided to start with the seller of fish.

"Your fish looks very good today," he said to the man while leaning on the table, head supported by one arm. "The mullet is nice and pink, and the barbel has a fine smell."

The man smiled. He wore a tunic of faded blue and red stripes, and he was busy cutting the head off a barbel. "You know fish very well," he said with a smile.

"My father was a fisherman," Bartholomew responded. The man didn't ask what had happened to Bartholomew's father but said instead, "Well, you are correct. This *is* very good fish today."

Now Bartholomew had the opening he'd been waiting for. "Do you think it is as good as the cheese of your neighbor?"

At this the man's smile faded, and he said through guilty lips, "How would I know such a thing?"

Bartholomew raised his eyes to the heavens. "Oh, I don't know . . . It seems that I saw something a short time ago that I'm starting to forget . . . ," and at this he started rubbing his temples, ". . . but hunger will not allow it to go away completely. Perhaps if I had a piece of smoked fish in my mouth I would forget all that I saw . . ."

The fish seller frowned. "So, it's extortion you want, eh! You'd force me to give you free fish in exchange for your silence?"

Now Bartholomew *really* had what he wanted. With a grin he looked right at the man. "No, I will not take fish if you think it extortion. But if you would think me your *friend* . . ."

The man stopped his cutting and looked at Bartholomew in surprise, which was exactly Bartholomew's plan. Then the man let out a loud laugh and cut off a piece of the smoked mullet. "A friend you shall be!" he said, handing the treat to Bartholomew on the end of his knife. "And what is your name?"

"Bartholomew of Taricheae."

"Well, Bartholomew of Taricheae, I am Mebach of Jericho, and I am honored to meet you." Then as Bartholomew munched on the smoked fish, the fish seller turned to the cheese seller next to him and slapped him on the arm. "Jethro!" he said, getting the man's attention, "this is my new friend, Bartholomew. Give him a piece of cheese!" Jethro looked a bit put out. "And why should I do such a thing?" he asked.

"Because if you don't," Mebach said loudly, "he's going to tell you that he saw me stealing a bite of your cheese earlier!"

Jethro looked completely confused at this but did as his friend said and cut Bartholomew a nice slice of goat cheese. He handed the cheese to Bartholomew as he slapped his fish-selling friend on the arm, and he said to Bartholomew, "May you find better friends than *this* old thief!"

Bartholomew grinned at the way the two played, and he knew he had found some new friends.

The sun had moved a tenth of the way across the sky when Bartholomew heard his name being called. Looking up from the seller of copper he had just met, he saw Nathan looking for him through the crowd. "Nathan! Here!" he called, running over to his friend.

Nathan spied the boy and said, "Come, now. Silas has prepared a fine meal."

Bartholomew rubbed his stomach and groaned. "Oh, I am so full I could not even eat a crumb of bread!" to which Nathan looked surprised.

But an hour later they had finished their breakfast, with Bartholomew eating enough to be polite. Then they packed their things to leave. With a hug that felt like that of a bear, Silas said goodbye to Bartholomew. "May our journeys cross again when Jehovah wills it so," the older man said.

"And may He grant us friendship forever," Bartholomew replied. Then he and Nathan were out the front door and making their way through the market.

"Goodbye, Bartholomew!" the seller of fish called across the square. Bartholomew waved, and Nathan smiled that the boy had made a friend already. Then Jethro the cheese seller waved and yelled his goodbye as well, and Nathan laughed, thinking how quickly his charge had made two friends. But then the seller of meat added his farewell to Bartholomew, as did the seller of perfumes and the seller of wine and the seller of bread and the seller of cloth, until just about the whole marketplace had stopped what they were doing to call their goodbyes. It was as if Bartholomew were some great and noble king walking through their midst. As each friend would yell to the boy, Nathan would spin this way and that to take it all in, looking as surprised as if he'd seen all the ghosts of his ancestors. As they reached the edge of the market and headed out through the gate in the city wall, Nathan wiped his forehead, looked at the boy, and said, "I did not know you had been to Jericho before!"

Bartholomew just kept looking straight ahead as they walked. "I have not," he said. "I just made friends with them this morning!"

The day wore on, and Bartholomew asked Nathan many questions as they walked. One of them was, "Why do you sometimes wear the hat of a fool?"

"We Essenes do not believe in violence," Nathan answered. "Yet, when I travel, I often encounter it. Playing the part of a fool allows me to fight for my safety—and that of others— without using violence."

Bartholomew thought about this awhile, then finally said, "My father would be grieved that I have not yet thanked you for saving me."

"A kind and proper thought," Nathan replied, "but you need not fret. Your father and I both know you have had much weightier things on your mind than being polite."

Bartholomew was silent for a few moments, then quietly asked, "Do you think my father and mother are alive?"

"Most assuredly," Nathan answered. "Your father and mother may be far away for now, but you shall see them again someday."

The way Nathan said it, so confident and matter-of-fact, helped ease the pain Bartholomew had felt in his heart for many days, and somehow his walking seemed to be just a bit easier after that.

The sun had traveled far across the sky, and Nathan and Bartholomew had traveled far along the road, when they rounded a corner where huge stands of date palms hugged the edges of the Jordan River. Then they saw a lake that Bartholomew was sure was ten times bigger than the Galilee.

"The Sea of Death," Nathan said at Bartholomew's gasp. "Though I have found it to be a most friendly body of water."

Bartholomew grinned. "Well, making friends is what I do best, so I guess it will be my friend too!"

A short time later Nathan and Bartholomew were walking along a point where the road was trapped between the Sea of Death on the left and a cliff that rose a thousand feet on the right. Suddenly, off in the distance, they heard rolling thunder. Only this time Bartholomew knew instantly that it was not thunder. "Romans!" he gasped, before he could even see around the corner.

Nathan must have thought so too, because he instantly started looking this way and that, trying to find a place to hide. But the road was so narrow and the cliff so steep that there was no place to go. A moment later Bartholomew saw four horses the size of elephants come charging around the corner, sweat flying from their pumping muscles and fright in their eyes as if they were being chased by demons. The four horses pulled a chariot of white and gold, and the chariot held a Roman centurion and his driver, red robes flying behind them like flags in the wind.

Bartholomew stared at the four beasts racing toward him, so close he could feel the pounding of their hooves on the ground, and he knew in an instant there was no way the driver could possibly stop the horses, even if he wanted to.

Bartholomew grew up believing that the Messiah would come as a great warrior to kill all His enemies. He believed this because so many people around him believed it and kept saying it. But as Nathan pointed out, the truth isn't always in what the majority of the people believe; it's in the Word of God.

Many people today believe that following God means following a set of rules. Don't do this, don't do that, and then you'll go to heaven. But God's Word tells us that what we *do* is not as important as *why* we do it. If we are selfish, if we do the things we do so we can get more for our*selves*, then we are being sinful. But if we follow God's example and try to live in unselfish love, then we are already following God's law.

Jesus came to earth partly to demonstrate such love for us. He didn't need to follow a bunch of laws in order to be godly. He just needed to care more about others than about Himself.

Jesus said:

> "'Love the Lord your God with all your heart and with all your soul and with all your mind.' This is the first and greatest commandment. And the second is like it: 'Love your neighbor as yourself.' All the Law and the Prophets hang on these two commandments." MATTHEW 22:37–40

It may not be what most of the world believes, but it's the most important thing that Jesus taught us.

And it's the most important thing we can ever know.

Qumran

Light the first two violet candles.

The driver of the chariot would have cared more about a dog in the middle of the road than he did a Jewish man and boy. He whipped the horses hard, driving them straight into Nathan and Bartholomew. Nathan leapt to the Dead Sea side of the road, grabbing Bartholomew by the tunic as he went. Man and boy landed in the water with a splash just as the wheels of the chariot sliced through their footprints on the road.

Bartholomew choked on the salty water and scrambled to his feet. Nathan stood next to him, dripping salt water, and then they noticed that the chariot, and four others behind it, were sliding to a stop. The centurion in the first chariot stepped off his mount even before it had stopped moving and marched over to the two travelers. With six soldiers falling in behind him, he stood on the edge of the road, looking down on Nathan and Bartholomew, whose appearance was that of wet laundry from a woman's wash bin.

"Your names," the centurion demanded, completely unconcerned that his chariot had almost run them over.

"Nathan of Hebron," Nathan answered in a strong voice, "and my son Matthew." The centurion eyed them for several seconds, then asked, "Where are you coming from, and where are you going?"

"We just finished a visit in Jericho," Nathan answered, "and are heading home."

"How long in Jericho?" the centurion asked, suspicion dripping off his tongue.

"We were there many days, ten at least."

"Then tell me," the centurion said slowly. "You must have seen many people that could witness for you, if you were there that long?"

Nathan's voice was just a little nervous as he said, "Why, yes, of course. Let me see, we stayed with our friend Silas—he's a merchant of many fine goods—then there was, uh, his friend Seth! An innkeeper! And then . . . let me see now . . ."

Suddenly Bartholomew jumped into the conversation. "Mebach the fish seller!" his high-pitched voice rang out. "Don't you remember, Father?"

"Oh, of course, Mebach!" Nathan said.

"And then there was Jethro, the dealer in cheese," Bartholomew continued, "and Solomon, the perfume maker, and Rachel, the spinner of wool, and Elias, who gave me this fine and precious ring." Bartholomew pulled a bronze ring from his pocket that had a shiny blue stone in the middle.

Nathan quickly gathered his wits and said, "Oh, yes, Elias. He was so kind to my son. Gave him that ring as a token of thanks for our business . . ."

Without missing a beat the centurion asked, "When did you leave Caesarea?"

If Nathan was fooled by the question, it didn't show on his face, nor did Bartholomew react in any way. "Caesarea?" Nathan exclaimed. "We were in Jericho, not Caesarea! Though I should like to visit that great city someday. I hear it is a magnificent work! Don't they call it 'Little Rome'?"

The centurion stared at Nathan for a moment, then said, "Yes, they do." He must have decided that these two were not who he was looking for, because he said, "A man posing as a fool stole a boy-slave from Caesarea four days ago. Do not make the mistake of helping them, should your paths cross."

"A slave-boy!" Nathan exclaimed. "Well, I do hope you catch him before he harms anyone!"

The centurion didn't say a word but just stared at Nathan for a long time, while Nathan tried to keep the fear from showing in his eyes. Then the Roman turned back to his chariot, and all five were gone in a cloud of dust. Nathan and Bartholomew both sat down in the water with a splash, their knees too weak to hold them up.

"A fine performance," Nathan said finally, his heart still racing.

"And yours also," Bartholomew panted.

"Where did you get that ring?" Nathan asked.

"From Elias, as I said. I traded him a prayer shawl for it."

"And where did you get a prayer shawl?"

"From Sarah, the seamstress. I traded her some perfumed ointment for it."

"And where did you get . . . oh, never mind," Nathan said. "I think this conversation could take a very long time indeed, and we must be on our way."

Some while later, as they walked along the road, their clothes having dried in the hot afternoon sun, Bartholomew said, "Nathan?"

"Yes, child," the man answered.

Bartholomew hesitated for a moment, then, without looking at his friend said, "It felt good to call you 'Father.'"

Nathan put his arm around the boy and pulled him close. Finally he said, "We shall someday soon find your mother and father. But until then, I would be proud if you would think yourself my son."

Bartholomew pulled close to Nathan, and the two walked together for a long time. "Does not the Torah tell us it is wrong to lie?" Bartholomew asked after a while.

"Almost," Nathan answered. "One of the ten laws Jehovah gave to Moses tells us we must not bear false witness."

"Did not we witness falsely to the centurion?" Bartholomew asked.

Nathan squirmed a bit. "Well, yes, but that was a different sort of thing."

"Different how?"

"Well," Nathan said, stalling, "we did not witness . . . that is, we were not trying . . ." Finally he let out a big sigh. "I shall have to think on these things. We will discuss them when my thoughts are clear."

A short time later Bartholomew started itching all over, as if a horde of ants had crawled under his clothes. He began scratching wildly. "What *is* this!" he cried. "What's happening?"

Nathan, too, was scratching. "It's the salt from the Sea of Death. The water is fine for swimming, but you must always rinse off in fresh water afterward. Otherwise the salt dries on your skin and . . . and does this!"

"How do we make it stop?" Bartholomew whined.

"We must bathe in cool, fresh water."

Bartholomew looked around but saw no stream or lake. "Where?!" he exclaimed.

"Just over that hill, I should think," Nathan answered. And as they crested the hill Bartholomew saw a large compound surrounded by a broken-down wall. There were many low buildings of stone and mortar. A canal that reminded Bartholomew of the aqueduct at Caesarea carried water right into the middle of the complex. Men and boys were busy working to rebuild the wall, while two men stood atop a tall tower keeping watch.

"Welcome to Qumran," Nathan said. "My home, and now yours."

They entered through the broken gate, and several of the boys ran up to Nathan as several of the men called their greetings. Bartholomew noticed that many of the men were wearing long white robes with hoods, and walked as if they were in mourning for a dead friend.

Nathan led the way to a large pool, where he and Bartholomew quickly rinsed off. The cool water felt good, and the itching stopped immediately. They rinsed their tunics as well, and, as Bartholomew was slipping his back on, he suddenly realized that, with all the people doing this and that, he didn't see any women.

"Nathan!" he whispered. "Where are all the women?"

Nathan laughed. "We Essenes devote our whole lives to learning about Jehovah," he said. "We study the Torah, pray, and work to preserve the words of Jehovah. We have no time for wives. As King Solomon said, 'It is better to live on the corner of the roof than to share a house with a quarrelsome wife!'"

Bartholomew scrunched up his face. "Didn't Solomon have *many* wives?"

"Exactly!" Nathan said. "Who would know better?" But then he added, "It is not forbidden for us to marry, and perhaps someday I shall. It would just be most inconvenient at present."

Bartholomew looked at the boys who had greeted Nathan and asked, "If you have no wives here, where did all the children come from?"

Nathan was just opening his mouth to answer when a loud voice filled the compound. "Nathan!" it said, and Bartholomew saw it came from a rather round-looking man with a bald head and red beard. "I heard the watchman call your approach and was surprised to hear of your return so soon!"

The heavy man waddled over to Nathan and Bartholomew, followed by a tall thin man.

The way the second man walked reminded Bartholomew of Hasbah, his slave master, but his face reminded him of the skunk man.

"My visit to Caesarea was shortened by some important business, Rabbi," Nathan said. The Rabbi looked from Nathan to Bartholomew, then a look came over his face like the look Bartholomew's father used to get when Bartholomew hadn't done his chores. "Oh, Nathan!" he cried. "Not *another* one!"

Bartholomew has raised a question that Nathan is finding most difficult to answer: Was it wrong for him to lie to the centurion? How do we know that a thing is right or wrong?

The answer seems to be that God has given us a simple test, the test of selfishness. Am I doing this thing for selfish or unselfish reasons? If a thing is done for unselfish reasons, then it probably is not wrong. For instance, Jesus healed a man on the Sabbath, even though it broke the religious rules of the day. By doing this he was showing us that the law of unselfish love is more important than any other law.

But God also gave us common sense, and sometimes we have to mix that with our unselfish love to find an answer. For instance, Jesus and His disciples picked some grain to eat on the Sabbath, even though there was a religious law against doing so. In this way He was showing us that common sense is sometimes more important than rules—our bodies require nourishment, and God never intended rules and laws to make us do foolish things.

Was it wrong for Nathan to tell the centurion something that wasn't true?

As we get ready to celebrate the birth of Jesus, this might be a good time to ask Him what He thinks. Ask Him to help you know what's right and what's wrong—and to always do the unselfish thing!

Rules

Light two violet candles and the pink candle.

Bartholomew, wake up!"

The command was coming from his new friend Andrew, Bartholomew knew, but he didn't want to listen.

"Bartholomew," the voice said again, "you must get up for morning prayers!"

This was Bartholomew's third day at Qumran, and it was beginning to feel like home, but he still didn't like getting up before the sun. He had done it back in Taricheae to help his father prepare the boats, but *that* was for *fishing*, not for going to boring old prayers.

Then, as his mind awoke and he opened his eyes, Bartholomew decided he was very lucky to be in Qumran at all. He would do whatever it took to stay there, because he had almost been forced to leave. After the Rabbi had realized that Bartholomew was not one of the boys already living in Qumran, he had become very upset.

"Nathan, this idea of yours to bring orphan boys into Qumran, well, it just is not going to work. While you were gone there were *three* incidents of boys talking during the evening meal. And yesterday loud laughter was heard coming from the boys' dormitory!" The Rabbi wiped his forehead with a cloth. "It was *most* distressing. Most distressing indeed!"

The Rabbi's assistant, arms folded inside the sleeves of his tunic, smirked at Nathan. Nathan ignored him as he spoke to the Rabbi. "If we follow only the *rules* of the Torah and not the *heart* of the Torah," he said, "are we not ignoring the *truth* of the Torah? Does not even our father Moses write that Jehovah 'defends the cause of the fatherless, giving him food and clothing'? And does not our father David say that the Lord watches over the fatherless but frustrates the ways of the wicked'?"

"Yes, yes, yes," the Rabbi said, "you have made all these arguments before. But I've been thinking," and here the Rabbi gave a glance at his assistant, who smirked again, "I've been thinking that these are the things that *Jehovah* does. They are not things He has told *us* to do."

Nathan started to protest that God did indeed command such things, but the Rabbi cut him off. "Yes, yes, yes," he said again, "I know your arguments, and you may keep the boy here for now. But know that I am considering this issue carefully, and my decision will be final!"

With that the Rabbi had walked away, but he turned back long enough to say, "Be sure the boy learns and follows the Manual of Discipline."

"As you say," Nathan said with a bow. Then he let out a quick breath and said absently, "That's getting harder every time."

"What is?" Bartholomew asked.

Nathan turned to the boy and smiled. "Nothing you need to worry about. All you need to know right now is the Manual of Discipline, and you had better learn it faster than any of the other boys have."

"Where did they all come from?" Bartholomew asked about the boys.

"Oh, here and there, wherever I've come across them in my travels. It seems that Jehovah has given me a special gift of helping young orphan boys in need!"

Bartholomew decided he was quite grateful that Jehovah had done such a thing and would thank Him in his prayers that evening.

"So," Nathan continued, leading the boy over to a room where rolls of leather lay on wooden tables, "the Manual of Discipline." Nathan found the roll he was looking for and unrolled an arm's length. The scroll was covered in blocky writing that Bartholomew did not recognize. "Do you know how to read?" Nathan asked.

"A little," the boy answered. "Only a few letters, really. My father was just beginning to teach me."

"Well, it would do you no good anyhow," Nathan said. "These rules, and most of the scrolls the Essenes write for themselves, are written in a secret language that no one outside our community understands."

Bartholomew twisted up his face. "Why do you do *that*?" he asked.

Nathan sighed. "The Essenes think that they are the chosen few of God and that any contact with the rest of the world—the sons of darkness—will soil them. They write in secret codes so no one who is not a member will know about their community."

"Why do you say *'they'*? Are not *you* an Essene?"

"Well, yes, I am," Nathan said, and Bartholomew could tell there was a fight going on inside his friend. "I believe it is a good thing to separate yourself from the world for a time, as the Essenes do, to spend time alone with Jehovah, to seek out His truth. But there are many things the Essenes believe that I cannot accept. I believe the words of Jehovah are meant for all people, not just a few men in the desert. That is why it is I who travels whenever the community is in need of some or another thing. I use those trips to spread the message of God's love. And," he said with a smile, "to collect a new orphan or two."

Bartholomew laughed aloud, then Nathan said, "And that is the first of the rules you must learn. Laughter in moderation is acceptable, but you must not laugh too loudly."

And with that Nathan began to read to Bartholomew from the Manual of Discipline.

That had been three days earlier, and in that time Bartholomew had learned many rules. No one was to speak before the morning prayers, he'd learned, and his friend Andrew had broken this rule to warn him to get out of bed. There could be no spitting during meetings and meals, the Manual said, and only fully initiated members could wear the white linen tunics and carry the small axes on their belts that the Essene members did. Everyone must work hard at his given job; bread and wine must first be touched by the priest before anyone else; no yelling in the compound; wash your hands and arms before every meal. The rules went on and on until Bartholomew thought his head could hold no more.

But two of the rules were especially bad, Bartholomew thought. Every day at the fifth hour, every member of Qumran had to take a bath. And it was a *cold* bath! A special pool had been built in one corner of the community, and all the men and boys would bathe at once, just as Nathan had done in Jericho, but in water so cold Bartholomew was sure it would really be ice if the Rabbi didn't have some magical spell. At home Bartholomew only had to take a bath once every new moon, and that was in the Galilee, where the cold didn't threaten to make your fingers and toes fall off. And as if a bath a day weren't bad enough, every day the Rabbi kept chanting long chants about how the cold water would purify their souls.

Bartholomew had decided he could live with the baths, however, if it just weren't for that *other* rule, the one that said they could eat only two meals a day, with nothing in between. "That's as bad as being a slave!" Bartholomew had lamented when Nathan read this rule. "I will surely starve to my death!"

But so far Bartholomew had kept death from his door by eating as much as he could possibly stuff into his mouth at every meal. Of course, no amount of food could keep Bartholomew's mouth from talking, and he was constantly being scolded to be quiet during the meals.

With all these rules spinning in his head, Bartholomew decided he had indeed better get out of bed, or he'd be breaking the rule about everyone attending every prayer and meeting. He shivered just a bit as he climbed out from under the warm blankets, and he quickly pulled on his new tunic, which was very plain and just like the ones worn by all the other boys. The tunic that Silas had given him was far too fancy for the simple life of the Essenes, he'd been told.

Bartholomew walked silently to the prayers and then stood in line to wash his hands and arms before going into the dining hall for breakfast. Here, at least, a fire burned in a special place in the wall, keeping the room warm.

At Bartholomew's first meal at Qumran, one of the leaders had asked him what line he was from. Bartholomew had no idea what that meant, so he had been placed at the very end of the last table, where "Visitors and the Sons of Dan" had to sit. Bartholomew's line had seemed very important to the Essenes, and several of them spent a long time quizzing Bartholomew about his father and his father's father and his father's father's father and so on.

So, on this morning, Bartholomew took his place where the lowest members of the community sat, and, like always, some of the boys sneered at him from the front of the table. Nathan had explained that this was mostly jealousy, because they, too, thought of Nathan as their friend and didn't like his bringing new boys to the community. Bartholomew couldn't understand this because he had many brothers and sisters and knew his parents had loved them all the same.

"The order shall come to order," the Rabbi droned with a rap on the table. Instantly everyone was silent. "Let us thank Jehovah for that which He alone has provided and which will sustain us in His service on this day." Bartholomew closed his eyes and followed the Rabbi's prayer intently, even though it was too long as always. Then he said, "Selah!" with the rest of the men and boys and started dishing up stew from a big bowl. A moment later he felt a hand on his shoulder and turned to see Nathan.

"Bartholomew," he said, "it is time to move."

Bartholomew's heart sank. He was just becoming accustomed to life in Qumran, and now he was going to have to leave. He sighed sadly. "Will I ever again have a home where I am wanted?"

Nathan looked perplexed, then stifled a laugh. "No, no, Bartholomew, you do not need to move from Qumran. You need to move to your rightful place at the tables. Pick up your bowl."

Bartholomew did as he was told, then stood and followed Nathan. Everyone stopped eating and watched as they walked past the men he had come to know at this end of the table, past the boys who sneered at him, past even the Rabbi's assistant, to the very front place of the very first table, right across from where Nathan and the Rabbi himself sat. There was an awed silence in the room as everyone turned to stare.

"Here, Bartholomew," Nathan said loudly, "this is your rightful place, as a son of Jehru, son of Eleazar, son of Zadok, son of Hezekiah, in the line of David!"

Despite any rules, the whole gathering gasped loudly, and whispers could be heard throughout the dining hall. Bartholomew didn't understand what it all meant, but he was glad to be sitting across from Nathan and happily took his new seat. The murmuring continued as the men and boys turned back to their eating.

It wasn't long, though, before Bartholomew was wishing he were back at his old place. Up here the Rabbi kept watching him, frowning at the way he held his spoon, clearing his throat loudly when Bartholomew picked up a piece of meat with his fingers. Finally the Rabbi leaned over to him and whispered, "Son of David, you must be perfect in your behavior. You are setting an example to all the others." Then, for the first time, a smile crossed the Rabbi's face. "Fear not, I shall teach you," he said, and Bartholomew wondered why he was deserving of all this new attention.

Then, as always, the Rabbi stood and began the lessons of the day, only now Bartholomew was so close that the Rabbi's loud voice hurt his ears. "In the desert prepare the way for the Lord," he rang out, "make straight in the wilderness a highway for our God," and all the assembly said, "Selah!"

"This is the session of the men of the Name," he droned on as he did at every meal, "invited to the feast for the council of the community, when God begets the Messiah to be with them. The priest shall come at the head of the whole congregation, and all the Sons of Aaron, invited to the feast of the men of the Name. They shall sit before him, each according to his rank . . ." And on and on the Rabbi read from the scrolls, not changing a word except when he got to a part where it said, "All men shall cleanse their minds by the truth of the statutes of God, and direct their energy according to the integrity of their ways . . ." In these places he would change "All men" to "All men *and boys*," emphasizing the "*boys.*"

Finally the Rabbi quit moaning. Bartholomew had stuffed as much stew into his belly as it could hold, and everyone left the dining hall to meet the sun, which had finally risen. Each went off to his various jobs, and it was then that Nathan came to Bartholomew.

"You received a high honor today, Bartholomew," he said.

Bartholomew shrugged. "I still don't understand."

Nathan laughed, though not too loudly. "Nor do I, child." Then he explained. "The Essenes think that Jehovah will order His heaven according to the birthrights of men. You and I are fortunate—we are direct descendants of King David. To the Essenes that makes us almost as important as the priests. But to me," Nathan said, "I don't believe it matters to Jehovah *whose* son you are. He cares only that there is love in your heart."

Bartholomew nodded. He thought that Nathan's version made much more sense than the Essenes'.

"I do have news," Nathan continued as they walked, and this perked up Bartholomew's ears. "I must leave today on a short trip to En Gedi. The Rabbi needs some supplies that I can get only there."

Bartholomew's shoulders dropped. "You're leaving?" he asked. "Can I go with you?"

"No, I'm afraid I cannot allow this. En Gedi is a dangerous place, and no place at all for a boy. It is safe only for thieves and cheaters," Nathan said. Then whipping out his fool's cap and pulling it down over his ears he added, "And fools!"

Bartholomew laughed at the sight but then turned serious again. "But what shall I do while you are gone?"

"Do your chores, take your baths, eat your meals, and before you know it I will return." But Nathan seemed to know that these were not the things on Bartholomew's mind. He seemed to know that Bartholomew was really asking, "Who will protect me?" So Nathan added, "Just stay close to Andrew and your other friends. And if there is trouble, run to the Rabbi. He seems to have a new respect for you," he said with a wink.

Bartholomew nodded but inside felt sad and scared. Finally he said, "You will return, won't you?"

Nathan smiled. "Of course I will. No thief or Roman has ever outwitted this fool, and none shall start now. Perhaps I'll bring you a small gift. A piece of sugarcane, perhaps, or a blanket that is your own. Or maybe," Nathan said with another wink, "a new friend."

Bartholomew laughed at this. "I like having new friends," he said. "And I won't be jealous if you bring one!"

They both laughed at the joke, then Nathan picked up his bag and headed for the main gate, where several men and some of the older boys were hauling big rocks up wooden ladders to repair the wall. "Farewell, Bartholomew," he turned and waved. "I shall soon return from En Gedi!"

And as Nathan walked out of sight, Bartholomew once again felt he was all alone in the world.

The Essenes thought that if they followed all their rules carefully, hid from the rest of the world, and spent their days in prayer and study, they would sit at the banquet table of Jehovah someday. Seated, of course, in ranking of their birthright.

How nice it is to know that all of us who have been forgiven of our sins—whether we're rich or poor; David's son or Fred's son; boy, girl, man, or woman—*all* of us will be seated someday at the banquet table of Jesus. Not because we've meticulously followed some rules, not because we were born into the right race or belong to the right church or have the right color of skin. Simply because God loves us!

Yes, as Nathan has decided for himself, it is a very good thing to spend much time praying, and seeking God, and studying His Word. But Jesus told us to be a *part* of this world without allowing its temptations to lead us into selfishness. And why would He say that? Why not just separate ourselves and live godly lives apart from the rest of our community?

So that we can tell everyone else that God loves them, too!

Friends

Light two violet candles and the pink candle.

As Nathan walked out of sight, Bartholomew knew he had better get to work. His job, assigned to him the first day, was to help in the pottery shed, a large room tucked away in one corner of the compound. Going there now, he greeted his boss, Ezra, an old monk who seemed to hate everything and everybody. Everybody except Bartholomew, that is, who had instantly found the one warm spot in an otherwise grumpy heart.

"Good day, Ezra," Bartholomew greeted the old man. "May I fetch you a hot ointment for your weary arms?" Bartholomew knew the potter had already been at work since before dawn, pumping the pottery wheel with his foot while molding globs of clay into pots with his hands.

"A most welcome relief that would be," Ezra said. His mouth was so used to frowning, Bartholomew had decided, that no amount of smiling could fix it. But when the monk looked up and saw Bartholomew, his frown was a little less obvious than usual.

Bartholomew fetched a dram of hot ointment from the apothecary and rubbed it on the old man's joints, which had probably made more pots than there are camels in all of Israel, he thought. Then he set to work at his daily tasks. His was the job of taking the newly formed pots over to the ovens, where another monk would bake them for several hours. Bartholomew had to be careful on the way to the ovens that he didn't damage the soft clay. After the pots were baked and cooled, he'd carry them to a storeroom at the other end of the compound.

Once finished, the tall, narrow pots were used by the copyists in the scriptorium to store copies of the Torah and other important documents. The scriptorium, Bartholomew had learned, was where several monks sat all day and made copies of the Torah. Once he had gotten to peek in the door for a few minutes and had seen how the leader guided the other monks in copying a book letter by letter.

Between the time he took the new pots over to the ovens and the time he picked them up again, Bartholomew had only to help Ezra clean up the pottery shed. Then he could do as he pleased. On this particular day it pleased him to make a new friend of the community's cook.

"Greetings," Bartholomew said as he entered the cook room from the dining hall. The short, plump monk in his hooded white linen robe was startled and almost dropped a large pot of water. "Oh, child!" he chastised. "Do not scare a man so!"

"I'm sorry," Bartholomew said with a bow. "Forgive my trespass, and allow me to make amends." This was something he had heard his father say often. He was never quite sure what "amends" were, but he figured he could make almost anything that could be made.

The monk waved a hand as he hung the pot over the fire pit. "Nothing to forgive, no trespass made," he said.

"Then let me make an amend anyway," Bartholomew said, and the cook-monk couldn't help but smile. "I just came in to tell you that your food makes my tongue sing the praises of Jehovah and sweetens my stomach like manna from heaven!"

The cook stopped stirring the water, to which he had just added some rice, and stared at Bartholomew. "Do you know you are the only boy to ever say such a thing?" he said finally. "Every day I slave away in here, steam in my face, sheep blood on my clothes, smoke in my eyes, and not one single boy of Nathan's has ever said so much as 'Thank you!'"

"I am sure they like the meals as much as I," Bartholomew said, "and just forget to tell you."

The cook started stirring again and said, "I care not for praise, but ask only a little appreciation." Then, turning to Bartholomew, he asked, "What is your name, boy?"

"Bartholomew of Taricheae. And what may I call you?"

"John of Qumran," he said. Then, after a moment's thought, "Would you care to try some fresh bread?"

The shadow on the sundial had moved a quarter mark when Bartholomew finally emerged from the kitchen, a belly full of bread and several taste-tests of stew keeping him company. Which had been exactly his plan. He liked to make friends just to make friends, but if it sometimes filled his belly, well, that was OK too. The rule about eating only two meals a day was a difficult one for many of the community, he had learned. But *his* stomach seemed to growl extra loudly without lunch.

Bartholomew's next stop was the scriptorium. The monks here got to rest a few minutes every two hours, to prevent mistakes from being made on the Torah out of weariness. He waited until such a break, then found the copyist he was looking for.

"Micah?" he said, and the monk, who was about the same age as Bartholomew's father, looked up.

"What is it, boy?" he asked gruffly.

"I have been told that you are the finest of all copyists, and that you read better than anyone in the camp."

The compliment seemed to have no effect on the monk, who said simply, "Yes, it is so. Why do you care?"

"I care because my father told me to seek out wise counsel whenever I am in need of learning."

"Tell your father he should teach you himself and not put his burdens on other men."

Bartholomew lowered his head and spoke softly. "My father was made a slave and taken to Rome," he said, then raised one eye to see what effect this had on the copyist.

"So was mine," the monk said abruptly. "And so are many people's. Now go your way so I may take my rest."

Bartholomew sighed and put on his saddest look. "Very well," he said. "I was hoping only for a . . . well, never mind. I'll leave you to your much-deserved rest. I have seen how hard you work and know of your great skill. Such mastery should not be disturbed by a ten-year-old boy."

The monk harrumphed at the words, and Bartholomew bowed deeply, then turned to go. But as he did he pulled from his tunic, such that Micah couldn't help but see, a big piece of fresh bread, still warm and smelling fresh and tempting. The copyist gasped and said, "Boy! Where did you get that?"

Bartholomew now put on his innocent look and said, "What? This piece of bread?"

"Yes, yes, of course," the monk hissed softly, looking around to see if anyone watched. "Do you not know it is forbidden to eat between meals?"

"Oh, I don't think of this as eating," Bartholomew said. "I just think of it as a gift from Jehovah so that I may better serve Him." Micah was staring at the bread, his mouth watering. Finally Bartholomew held out the bread and asked, "Would you not serve Jehovah better with a stomach that does not complain?"

The monk looked around carefully. Most of the other copyists were lying in the sun, their eyes closed against fatigue, or lined up to get drinks from a well. Seeing that no one was looking, he snatched the bread from Bartholomew's hand and scarfed it down in three bites. Wiping the crumbs from his mouth he said flatly, "What is it you want?"

"I shall bring you bread every day," Bartholomew answered, "so that your stomach will not hate you. I want nothing in return and will never ask anything of you. But," he said softly, "if you would be my friend and teach me to read, you will have the gratitude of my father."

Finally the copyist's mouth formed a small smile. "I have been selfish and cruel with you," he said. "It would be my honor to carry your father's burden in this thing. We will begin tonight for one hour before dinner."

Bartholomew's grin seemed to stretch from one side of the camp to the other. "May a thousand camels find their way to your corral," he said with a bow, "and may the Rabbi grant you leave to see your family."

Micah was shocked that Bartholomew knew of his request to the Rabbi, but he simply returned the bow and said, "It is time for me to return to my table." He started to turn away, but then faced Bartholomew once again. "And, please, there is no need to bring me bread. Grant me the honor of helping you without breaking the Rabbi's rules."

Bartholomew thanked the man for his generosity, then left. Ezra was still working, so Bartholomew decided to carve himself a walking stick. After walking so far on so many roads, he had decided he'd never walk again without a fine stick to help him.

A while later Bartholomew went to find Andrew. His friend was just finishing up his own chore of mixing mortar for the workmen, and the two decided it was a good time for a swim.

The Sea of Death was a strange place, as Bartholomew had discovered when he and Nathan had jumped in to escape the chariots. The water was all slimy and slick and made Bartholomew's skin itch when he dried off, but he liked the way the water did not allow him to sink. Trying to see who could stay under the longest was their favorite game, because the water kept trying to push them back up. This was because of the salt in the water, Nathan had told him, and Bartholomew spent many hours trying to figure it out.

Andrew and Bartholomew splashed each other and played Dunk the Donkey for a good long time, then finally waded out of the water to where they had left their clothes on some rocks.

Their tunics were gone.

Standing there with no clothes on, shivering in the wind, the boys were about to run back up to Qumran when the three oldest boys in the community stepped around the rocks. They were holding the boys' tunics up on sticks, and they also held hand-sized stones. Slowly the three big boys surrounded the two smaller ones. "So, Nathan's little baby doesn't have Nathan to protect him," the oldest boy sneered. "Want your clothes, little boy?" he asked sarcastically. "Well, then, come and get them!"

Why do so many adults look down on children and teenagers? Sometimes it's just because that adult is bitter inside. But sometimes it's because many teenagers and children have not yet learned to be unselfish. They want what *they* want, with no care about how that might affect others.

But many times children and teenagers have low opinions of adults, too. Usually it's because they've seen some adults acting in very selfish ways.

How do we overcome these stereotypes? First, by being sure that we are not treating others with disrespect by acting selfishly.

"Honor your father and mother." MATTHEW 15:4

And then by showing them the love inside us that comes from the Messiah.

Don't let anyone look down on you because you are young, but set an example for the believers in speech, in life, in love, in faith and in purity.

1 TIMOTHY 4:12

Bartholomew has learned that treating adults with respect and honesty can earn him their friendship. Micah has learned that children need an extra special amount of care. Maybe they have both already learned the lesson that Jesus came to earth to bring—the lesson that unselfish love is God's answer for most everything!

Jotham's Journey

Light two violet candles and the pink candle.

Bartholomew looked at his tunic hanging on the end of the stick. He knew that if he reached for it the older boy would just pull it away. Then they'd all gang up on him and beat him up.

On the other hand, he knew he could not get through the circle of older boys, and even if he did they would catch him. And beat him up.

And if he just stood there and did nothing, he figured, they'd finally get tired of waiting. And beat him up.

None of these options seemed too pleasant. Andrew must have figured this out too, because he started whimpering quietly beside Bartholomew. The older boys laughed. "Cry, little Andrew!" they chanted.

Finally Bartholomew had had enough. He pulled himself up straight, sucked in a deep breath, and looked straight in the gang leader's eye. "How many camels does it take to carry a rabbi?"

The boys stopped laughing, stopped taunting Andrew, stopped doing *any*thing, and just stared at Bartholomew in confusion.

Finally the leader screwed up his face and said, "What?"

"I said, how many camels does it take to carry a rabbi?"

By now the older boys were completely baffled. "I don't know," their leader said flatly.

"Three," Bartholomew said. Then he waited until the other boy asked, "Why three?"

"One to carry his body," Bartholomew said, "one to carry his soul, and one to carry his wisdom." The other boys, including Andrew, just looked at him with a "What are you *talking* about?" look. Bartholomew plunged ahead.

"How many camels does it take to carry a rabbi's *assistant*?" he asked. This time the leader just shook his head mutely. "Three," Bartholomew said again. "One to carry his body, one to carry his soul, and one to carry the skunk whose face he stole!"

The boys stared at Bartholomew, then the lips of the leader started to curl upward a bit—just a fraction at first, but then more and more until he was grinning. And then he started laughing, and so did the other two boys as they got the joke, and so did even Andrew. In a moment all three of the bullies were rolling on the ground holding their stomachs, laughing so hard they were crying. When the oldest of the three had calmed down enough, he asked Bartholomew, "Did you find that joke in your travels, or did you think of it yourself?"

"Oh, it just popped into my head," Bartholomew said innocently, "the first moment I saw the Rabbi's assistant!"

This brought another burst of laughter, as the boys all agreed that the Rabbi's assistant did indeed look like a skunk. Finally, the leader stood to his feet and held out his hand. "I am Jacob," he said, still laughing a bit, "son of Joab, son of Ethan."

"Bartholomew, son of Jehru," Bartholomew said, grasping the other boy's forearm.

Jacob lowered his head and looked at the ground. "I ask your forgiveness for my trespass," he said solemnly.

"I saw no trespass," Bartholomew answered. "I saw only a friend holding my tunic for me."

Jacob looked up and grinned. "And a friend you shall be."

The other boys introduced themselves and also apologized. A short while later, they all walked back to the compound, chanting, "One for his body, one for his soul, one for the skunk whose face he stole." After Bartholomew and Andrew rinsed off in the pool, the boys and their new friends sat in a courtyard around a square stone with etchings in it and played a game of King's Ransom.

For four days Bartholomew did his chores, got snacks from John, met with Micah for reading lessons, and made friends with all the other boys in Qumran. At the fifth hour he'd bathe with everyone else, in the morning and evening he'd attend prayers, and at meals he'd listen to the Rabbi droning on and on, and usually get in trouble for talking when he wasn't supposed to be. And one time he tried to ask the Rabbi about the Messiah's coming birth, but the Rabbi became very upset and started shouting that the Messiah wouldn't come for many years, and that Nathan must have been spreading lies again, and how he'd have to talk to Nathan when he returned.

Then, on the afternoon of the fourth day, as he was playing yet another game of King's Ransom with Jacob and his other new friends, Bartholomew heard the watchman in the tower cry out, "Travelers approaching!" Everyone stopped playing and stopped working and stopped studying to stare at the watchman high above them, waiting to hear if danger had come to visit. But then the watchman announced, "All is well. It is Nathan, returning from En Gedi."

Bartholomew's heart leapt at the words, but he had three jackals to Jacob's two goats and was about to win the game. It was Bartholomew's turn, so he threw the black and white sticks down onto the etched stone. The number of white sticks touching squares with stars was twelve, so Bartholomew's jackals ate Jacob's goats, and Bartholomew got to save the king, winning the game. He was just jumping up in celebration when Nathan approached, his arm around a young boy.

"Bartholomew," Nathan said, "this is our new friend Jotham." Bartholomew looked at Nathan with a smile in his eyes that said, "So you really *did* bring me a gift of a new friend!" Nathan added, "Why don't you introduce him to Qumran?"

Bartholomew bowed slightly and said, "It would bring me great honor." Then leaning over to Nathan he whispered, "I'll keep him away from the Rabbi."

"Good idea," Nathan whispered back.

"Come this way," Bartholomew said to Jotham, and the new boy followed him. Jotham was about the same size as Bartholomew. He looked enough like Bartholomew that they could be brothers, except that Jotham looked as if he were used to working outside. He was wearing a tunic so big that he looked like a baggy elephant in it.

"Are you an orphan?" Bartholomew asked, politeness not allowing him to comment on the size of the boy's tunic.

Jotham shrugged his shoulders. "I do not know . . . I do not think so."

"Then where is your family?"

Again Jotham shrugged and said, "I do not know. I lost them many days ago and have been searching the desert for them."

"How do you lose a whole family?" Bartholomew asked, his eyes wide in amazement.

Jotham was silent for a few moments. Then he said quietly, "I did a bad thing and ran away into the hills. When I returned, my family had left. They thought I was dead."

"Your family moved to a new town just because they thought you dead?" Bartholomew gasped, thinking how his own family would have stayed in Taricheae to mourn.

"My father is a shepherd," Jotham said sadly. "It is our way."

Bartholomew understood now. He also understood the sadness in his new friend, so he changed the subject. "This is our dormitory," he said, pointing to the long building with three windows. Then, seeing this was a new word for Jotham, he added, "The place where we sleep. Perhaps Nathan will allow you to place your mat next to mine."

"I would like that," Jotham said, a smile finally finding his face.

"And this is the scriptorium," Bartholomew said as they continued along the compound. Seeing that this was *another* new word for Jotham, Bartholomew said, "Come inside. I'll show you."

Quietly the two boys stepped inside the dark of the scriptorium. Bartholomew showed Jotham the many monks sitting at tables copying the Torah, as a leader read it letter by letter. Jotham was amazed. Bartholomew slipped Micah a piece of bread, then the boys returned to the bright sunlight. Bartholomew explained the whole process, finishing with, "In this way we will have thirty new copies of the Torah in just two years!"

"Two *years*!" Jotham gasped.

"Yes," Bartholomew said smugly. "It is truly a modern-day miracle. When the copyists have written a book, the scrolls are placed in the urns that I help to make."

Jotham looked as if these ideas were all very strange, and at just that moment Nathan returned. "Jotham, I have a new tunic for you to wear," he said. Jotham gladly stripped off the old, oversized tunic and put on the new one, which fit just fine. Then a yell was heard across the compound.

"Nathan!" came a sharp cry. It was the Rabbi, storming across the compound toward Nathan like a bull charging a lion. "Nathan!" he called again.

"Yes, Rabbi, what is it?" Nathan said innocently as the Rabbi huffed and puffed his way over.

"You know *exactly* what it is!" the Rabbi said as he walked up. "You have once again been spreading your tales of the Messiah against my specific orders!" Then the Rabbi saw Jotham for the first time and added, "I'd wager you've even told this young boy here!"

Nathan sighed deeply. "Rabbi," he said evenly, "I spread no tales except those that are clearly told in Scripture."

The Rabbi's face turned purple and Bartholomew thought his head might pop like a grape. "Now see here, Nathan! I was studying the Scriptures before your parents ever laid eyes on each other, and I know perfectly well they say nothing of the tales you spread! The Messiah *will* come to us, but we must tarry for many generations before we are worthy of His arrival!"

Now Nathan began to turn red and Bartholomew knew this could be a long debate. "We don't *need* to be worthy," Nathan said, his voice beginning to rise. "We can *never* be worthy! The whole purpose of the Messiah is to cleanse us in our unworthiness!"

The argument went back and forth for several minutes, and Bartholomew wondered if he ever *would* get to talk to Jotham. Nathan kept trying to point out what the Scriptures said about the Messiah coming, and the Rabbi kept arguing that the people had to become perfect before the Messiah would appear. All the while the Rabbi's assistant stood back smiling, obviously pleased at Nathan's predicament.

"Nathan," the Rabbi said finally, "I am in charge here, and you *will* do as I say or face discipline from the council of elders!"

"Discipline!" Nathan exploded. "Discipline! For reading the Scriptures and seeing in them the truth?"

The Rabbi started to answer but was interrupted by an alarm from the watchtower.

"Riders!" was the cry. "Five men on horses riding fast from the south!"

Nathan's eyes widened, and he looked at the Rabbi, the argument of a moment ago forgotten. "Decha of Megiddo," he gasped. "I saved this boy from his clutches in En Gedi, and now he comes for him. I did not believe he would care enough to look this far."

The Rabbi's face melted into concern and compassion. Looking at Jotham he said, "You must take the boy to the hills and hide quickly!" Before Bartholomew could even say good-bye, the Rabbi led Nathan and Jotham toward the back of the compound.

Moments later, through the main gate, rode the man Bartholomew had seen and feared on his own trip to Qumran. Black robes billowed in the wind, and dust filled the air as Decha and his four henchmen slid their horses to a stop. The Rabbi returned from the back of the compound, breathing hard and sweating so much it looked as if he'd been swimming. He waddled quickly over to Decha, folded his hands in front of him as if he were praying, looking as innocent and helpful as possible. "Welcome, friend," he said.

"We're looking for a fool and a boy," Decha roared.

The Rabbi shook his head slowly. "No, no, we have no one here like that."

With no warning, Decha punched the Rabbi hard, knocking him over backward. The Rabbi landed with a thud, and Decha leaned over toward him. "Your lies will cost you your head!" Decha screamed, and all the monks and boys who had been gathering around to see what was happening suddenly began to shrink back.

"No, I assure you!" the Rabbi sputtered. "We are a peaceful community. Most of us do not ever leave this place. We seek only God and certainly have no fools here!"

So sincere was the Rabbi's voice that Bartholomew began to think that maybe he really didn't know that Nathan sometimes dressed as a fool.

Decha surveyed the compound, looking for a clue. "I will burn this place to the ground if I find you are lying!" he said. "And I will kill every man and boy who does not cooperate!"

At this the monks and most of the boys started slipping into doorways and alleyways, trying to hide from the evil that had invaded their home. Bartholomew himself slid into the shadows of an alcove.

Decha pointed at his henchmen. "You two! Search every corner of this place. Tear it down, if you have to. And you two, go out the back gate and search the hills!"

At this Bartholomew's heart fell. He knew that Nathan and Jotham hadn't had enough time to reach safety, and that the henchmen would surely see his friends once outside the walls. With a gulp as dry as the desert sands, he forced himself to leave the alcove and run out into the compound, just as the henchmen were getting ready to kick their horses into action.

"Kind sir!" Bartholomew yelled at Decha. "Kind sir!"

"What is it, boy?" Decha bellowed, seeing at once that this was not the boy he searched for.

"Kind sir! I have news!" Bartholomew said. The Rabbi looked as shocked as Bartholomew felt, because Bartholomew had no more idea than the Rabbi what he was about to say next.

"What news does a boy have that would interest Decha of Megiddo?" Decha roared.

"I, uh, heard a story! Yes, that's it!" Bartholomew said. "I heard a story about a fool and a boy!"

Decha was still impatient, but Bartholomew had caught his attention. "Speak your story," Decha said.

"The fool and the boy! They escaped from Caesarea, and the Romans are chasing them! The boy was a slave who ran away!"

"And where did you hear such a story?" Decha asked, with so much interest that Bartholomew wished he'd stayed back in the alcove. Suddenly he realized he didn't have a good answer for that question.

"Uh . . . uh . . ." Bartholomew stammered.

"Where, boy?" Decha shouted, and it echoed off the walls of Qumran.

"Uh, I heard it in Jericho! Before I came to this place." The Rabbi looked at Bartholomew in shock, and Bartholomew himself wondered where this story would lead. "I had many friends there," Bartholomew offered weakly, and he wondered if this would be a good time to tell his camels-and-the-rabbi joke.

Decha looked at the boy for a long moment, and when he had worked through all the thought processes he said, "The boy I search for was no slave. And he met the fool only last night."

Thus Decha dismissed Bartholomew and turned back to his henchmen.

"Go!" he ordered, but once again Bartholomew interrupted.

"I have a secret!" Bartholomew yelled, and once again the henchmen stopped in mid-kick. Decha drew a deep breath, then let it out sharply.

"A secret that delays Decha of Megiddo had best be of great importance," he growled, "or its teller will find himself missing a tongue!"

Decha looked straight into Bartholomew's eyes as he said the last of this, and Bartholomew felt as if he were staring into the face of a snake.

And he hoped his secret would be important enough.

What's going to happen next year? Could I have predicted or planned a year ago for the things that have happened since then? How can I best arrange things so that I can be as happy as God desires me to be?

No one knows the future, and no one can possibly plan for everything that might happen. And if we try to live our lives apart from God, there is no way we can make all the right choices to find such happiness. In fact, most choices we make apart from God lead only to disappointment or worse.

But just as Bartholomew is able to look some bullies in the eye and make friends of them, God is able to take the difficulties and disasters in our lives and make golden opportunities of them.

> And we know that in all things God works for the good of those who love
> him.   ROMANS 8:28

We do have to plan for our futures and prepare for the coming years. But in all our decisions we have two choices: Try to be our own gods and make the choices we *feel* like making, or let the one true God be Lord of our lives, and seek His counsel in all things. "I don't know what the future holds," the saying goes, "but I know who holds my future."

If we will trust in the Jesus of Advent, and the Father who sent Him, we will know greater joy and happiness than anything we could possibly have planned for ourselves. And more than that, we'll be ready when evil unexpectedly rides into our lives.

Decha

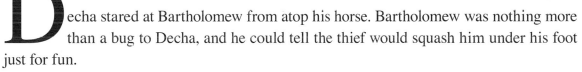

Light two violet candles and the pink candle.

Decha stared at Bartholomew from atop his horse. Bartholomew was nothing more than a bug to Decha, and he could tell the thief would squash him under his foot just for fun.

"Well," Decha growled, "what's this secret?"

Bartholomew's mind scrambled for an answer, but no great secret came to mind. He was trying to stall, of course. Anything to give Nathan and Jotham time to get into the caves in the hills. Finally Bartholomew looked at the Rabbi, and that gave him an idea.

"The Messiah is born!" he shouted at Decha.

The Rabbi looked shocked, but Decha just looked bored. He turned to his two henchmen and said, "Move out!"

Bartholomew ran alongside the horsemen as they trotted through the compound, yelling, "No! Wait! It is true! The Messiah is born, and He is here to show you God's love!"

The two henchmen laughed, then kicked their horses into a gallop and rode out the back gate. Bartholomew stood in their dust, watching them go, and hoped he had delayed them long enough.

Decha then ordered everyone to come out in the open compound, where he searched every face, while his other two henchmen searched every corner of every building. They didn't find what they were looking for, of course, and Decha seemed satisfied for the moment. All the monks and boys had to sit in the dirt, then, under the hot sun, waiting for the men in the hills to return. Bartholomew looked at all the men sitting in the compound—as many as a good catch of fish—then he looked at the three men who were guarding them and

111

wondered why they didn't all just gang up on the thieves and tie them up. But none of the monks moved, so Bartholomew just sat and worried, his stomach feeling as if it were sick. First the Romans had taken his father and mother, and now some Jews were trying to kill his *new* father. *Why does life have to be so full of hatred?* he wondered.

Sweat was running down Bartholomew's back, and stinging bugs flew around his head and bare arms. He kept looking at the pool in the middle of the compound, thinking he'd trade just about anything for a drink right now. He was just about to suggest a rebellion to the monk sitting next to him when the sound of hoofbeats came from the hills behind him. A moment later the two henchmen galloped through the gate and slid to a stop next to Decha.

The five thieves stood in a circle, talking softly, and Bartholomew saw a look of disappointment cross Decha's face. Decha looked up at the sun, then around at the compound. He announced in a loud voice, "We will stay here for the night and in the morning resume our search!"

The news that the thieves would be staying made Bartholomew's heart sink, but the news that they would continue their search meant that they had not found Nathan and Jotham, and this made his heart soar. Decha ordered all monks and boys to go back to their work, which is what they did, after lining up at the well to guzzle some water.

Dinner that night was a long and silent affair, and even Bartholomew didn't say a word throughout the meal. The Rabbi gave a short lesson and said the evening prayers right there at the table, then everyone went straight to bed. Bartholomew couldn't sleep, though, worried as he was about his friends. He lay there, staring out the window, asking Jehovah over and over to take care of Nathan and the new boy Jotham.

Suddenly a bright star appeared, brighter than any other, brighter even than the moon. Bartholomew had never seen a star appear before—they always just hung in the night sky and did not move. He jumped up and stuck his head out the window, leaning far out and craning his neck to see this wondrous sight. He looked back in the dormitory room to see whom he might share this event with, but all the other boys were asleep.

"Jehovah," he whispered to the sky as he turned back to the window, "if you can place a star like that in the heavens, then I think you can protect the lives of my friends." And with that he quit worrying, lay down, and went to sleep.

The sun had already risen when Bartholomew's eyes opened again, and he jumped up like a grasshopper. *I missed the morning prayers!* he thought, knowing his punishment would be great. But then he noticed that all the other boys were in the room as well, some of them sleeping, but most of them looking out the windows. Bartholomew wedged himself in between Andrew and Jacob. He saw, in the middle of the compound, Decha and his four henchmen on their horses. Decha was talking to the Rabbi.

"Forget not my warning," he was saying. Then louder, he looked up and spoke to all the men and boys hiding behind the doors and windows around the courtyard of the compound. "Forget not that I will kill any man who helps the fool and the boy!"

With that, Decha and his henchmen heeled their horses into action and bolted through the front gate. With the rest of the boys, Bartholomew hurried out of the dormitory and up a ladder to the roof of the scriptorium, where they could see Decha riding south, back toward En Gedi.

Now the whole community poured into the compound, everyone buzzing about the visit of Decha and no one caring that they were talking before morning prayers. Even the Rabbi was babbling on and on about Jehovah saving them. Finally he called for attention.

"Jehovah has brought us through a terrible ordeal," he sang out. "We shall gather in the prayer room for morning prayers to thank Him properly. But first, I must fetch our brethren who yet hide themselves in the library."

Then, with his assistant following in step, the Rabbi waddled out the back gate of Qumran toward the hills. A short time later he returned, red-faced and fuming, with Nathan and Jotham alongside. Nathan was just saying, "Woe to the prophets of Israel who watch out only for themselves!" and Bartholomew could tell they were in the middle of yet another debate about the boys.

The Rabbi turned purple and said, "You . . . I . . . Oh, never mind!" then stomped off toward the prayer room. Nathan looked at the Rabbi's assistant, who was scowling, and stuck out his tongue at him. The assistant was shocked, then infuriated, and stomped off after the Rabbi.

Bartholomew ran over to Nathan and hugged him tightly, as did Andrew and Jacob and a dozen other boys, until it seemed as if Nathan would be crushed. "I am so glad you are alive," Bartholomew said. "I prayed to Jehovah for you, and for you!" he said, looking at Jotham.

"All is well," Nathan said. "Jehovah has indeed seen fit to watch over us."

After morning prayers, a cold breakfast was served, then everyone went to work. Jotham helped Bartholomew carry the new urns to the furnace, then Bartholomew suggested a swim in the Sea of Death.

"You swim in the Sea of Death?" Jotham gasped.

"Of course," Bartholomew replied. "They are strange waters but most enjoyable. You will be safe."

Jotham felt desire in two directions—to go swimming but to stay as far away from the Sea of Death as possible. Finally the first desire won out, and he agreed to go. "But you must promise me I will come out alive!" he told his friend.

"I promise," Bartholomew answered with a grin. "But if you'd like, we can go ask the Rabbi's assistant if the water is safe."

Jotham looked horrified. "No, no, I believe you," he said. "I would not want to talk to that skunk-faced man!"

The two boys ran out the front gate, but before they got far they were stopped by a call from Nathan. "Jotham, I must speak with you," he said.

"Come swimming as soon as you can," Bartholomew told his friend, then ran down to the shores of the Dead Sea. He stripped off his tunic and dove into the water, the salty brine cooling his sunbaked flesh. Andrew, Jacob, and several other boys soon joined him, and they laughed and splashed as they played Dunk the Donkey.

A short time later Bartholomew saw Nathan and Jotham walking toward the water's edge. "Jotham! Come swimming!" he invited.

But then he noticed that his friend did not look very happy.

If you don't have God on your side—if you're living in a selfish way and trying to be Lord of your own life—then it's probably a pretty good idea to cower in the shadows whenever trouble comes your way. After all, if you're trying to be your own god, the only power you have to call on when you need help is your own. For most of us, that's not a great deal of comfort.

But if Jesus truly is the Lord of your life, if you're trying your best to seek Him and follow Him and live His law of unselfish love, then you can face troubles boldly, knowing that God is with you no matter the outcome. That's not to say we should *tempt* evil or *taunt* the devil, but when faced with a situation that is dangerous or unpleasant or tempting, we can look it straight in the eye and know that God is in control.

Like David fighting Goliath, we can stand tall and straight and say,

> "You come against me with sword and spear and javelin, but I come against you in the name of the LORD Almighty." 1 SAMUEL 17:45

We can say "No!" when faced with temptations that we know are wrong. We can say "No!" when asked to do something we don't believe is right. We can say "No!" when others try to hurt our friends and family.

Bartholomew couldn't understand why dozens of monks just sat and let evil men hunt down their friend. So Bartholomew himself bravely took action. Whose faith was greater? Which will control *your* life—fear or faith?

Discipline

Light two violet candles and the pink candle.

Jotham looked at Nathan, who nodded, then he stripped off his tunic. Before wading into the water he tested it with his toe. He pulled his toe out again, examined it closely, saw that it was not dead, then stepped into the water. As soon as he was waist deep, he floated up off the bottom of the lake and fell backward. Splashing and gagging he sputtered, "What's happening!"

Bartholomew and the other boys laughed, having gone through this themselves the first time. "It is the salt in the water," Bartholomew said as Jotham finally paddled himself upright. "There are so many grains of salt in the water that they stack up on top of each other and won't let you sink." It was a perfectly logical explanation, and Bartholomew was quite sure it was true, even if he had made it up himself. Jotham just stared into the water for a moment, then shook his head.

The other boys taught Jotham how to play Dunk the Donkey, and he got pretty good at being the donkey and being dunked, though the object of the game was to *not* be the donkey and *not* get dunked. Then the boys floated on their backs, allowing the thick water to hold them up, and rested in the sun.

"I have to leave tomorrow," Jotham said sadly. Bartholomew upended himself with a splash and twisted around to look his friend in the face.

"Leave! Why would you want to leave?"

"I must go to find my family," Jotham answered.

"But you don't know where your family is! You said they are lost and could be *any*where!"

"This is true. But they do not know I am alive, and if I do not look for them, we will never find each other."

Bartholomew was sad and lay back down in the water. "I will miss you, Jotham of Jericho," he said.

"And I you," Jotham answered. "But I will visit you again, as soon as I find my family and we travel this way."

Bartholomew didn't talk as the boys climbed out of the water, then rinsed off in a pool just inside the gate. He thought it strange when he saw the Rabbi's assistant gallop out of the compound on a horse and head in the direction that Decha had taken, but he was too distracted to think much of it. He was still silent as he pulled on his tunic a few minutes later.

"Are you sad?" Jotham asked.

Bartholomew's jaw moved back and forth a few times, and his lips were closed tight. "I am angry," he said finally.

"Angry at me?"

"No," Bartholomew answered. "I am angry at God. Because everything that is important to me keeps being taken away!"

"How can you be angry at God?" Jotham gasped. "Will He not strike you dead?"

Bartholomew turned his head away. "Sometimes I do not care," he said.

Jotham waited a time, then asked, "What happened to your family?"

Bartholomew was quiet for a long moment as they walked toward the dining hall, then said, "It started one afternoon, as I was drying my father's nets . . ."

A short time later the two boys had washed their hands and were waiting to enter the dining room as Bartholomew finished his story. "Then Nathan brought me here to Qumran, and I guess this is where I will stay until I am a man. Unless the Rabbi's assistant has his way."

"And you think God stole your family from you?"

Bartholomew sighed. "No, not really. But sometimes I get mad, and I don't know who to get mad at except God. And the Romans."

Everyone was entering the dining hall and taking their places now, and Bartholomew knew that, as a visitor, Jotham would have to sit at the end of the last table with the Sons of Dan. He looked around and spotted Nathan.

"Wait here," he told Jotham, then went over to his mentor. "Nathan," he whispered, "may I sit in my old place, to keep company with Jotham of Jericho?"

Nathan frowned. "Such a thing would be most unusual. An Essene does not give up his place of birthright for any reason. Such an act might cause a great disturbance among the people." Then Nathan smiled widely and whispered, "Of course you may do it!"

Bartholomew grinned back, then led Jotham to the place of visitors and sat. As dinner was served and consumed, Nathan began reading a lesson about the Messiah being from the line of Judah. Suddenly Bartholomew's curiosity tickled him. Leaning over to Jotham he whispered, "What line are you from?"

"What?" was Jotham's reply.

"I said, what *line* are you from?" Bartholomew whispered again.

Jotham looked puzzled. "I don't think I'm from *any* line!"

This caught Bartholomew completely off guard, and he let out a loud laugh and exclaimed, "You *have* to be from *some* line!"

Instantly Bartholomew realized his mistake. Everyone had stopped eating and was silently staring straight at him.

"For . . . forgive me, Nathan," he said lamely. "I was just trying to make our new friend feel welcome."

The Rabbi looked at Bartholomew with a sour-lemon face. "I shall speak with you after the meal, Bartholomew," he said.

Bartholomew nodded. He sat glumly through the rest of dinner, wondering what his fate would be. It didn't take long to find out. As soon as the meal was over, the Rabbi took Bartholomew by the ear and led him to the shed where wood for the cook fires was stored.

"Bartholomew," he said with the same voice Bartholomew's father had used when he did something wrong, "I have warned you many times about your outbursts during meals. I must now take a more drastic measure to help you remember!"

With that the Rabbi swung Bartholomew over his knee and spanked him, but, unlike in Caesarea, this time the punishment was real, and Bartholomew didn't have to pretend to cry. When he was done, the Rabbi set Bartholomew back on his feet and held him by the shoulders.

"Never forget, Bartholomew, that a man must live by the rules of the community or face the consequences." Then, letting loose of the boy, he said, "You may go now." Bartholomew was halfway to the door when the Rabbi called after him, "Just a moment. Why were you not sitting in your rightful place tonight?"

After explaining to the Rabbi, Bartholomew went out into the compound, where he found Jotham standing with a blank look on his face. Bartholomew was still sniffling as he said, "The Rabbi wanted to make sure I remembered not to talk during teachings."

Jotham just looked at him dumbly, as if he hadn't heard a word. "I am related to the Messiah," he said softly, as if he had seen an angel.

Bartholomew just laughed, although softly. "No, you are not!" he said.

Jotham nodded his head quickly. "Yes, yes, I am! Nathan himself told me this thing!"

Bartholomew stopped laughing. "But how can that be? The Messiah is . . . is God! No one can be related to God!"

"The Messiah will be from the line of Judah, just as I am!" Jotham exclaimed. Then, seeing that his friend did not understand, he asked, "Did you not listen to the lesson tonight?"

Bartholomew lowered his eyes to the ground. "Well, *most* of it," he said.

"But you did not hear the part where the Messiah will be born from the line of Judah?" Jotham asked. Then, before his friend could answer, he added, "What line are *you* from?"

"I am from the line of David," Bartholomew answered quickly, glad to be on a different subject. "But I don't really know what that means."

Jotham just stared at his friend for a moment. "It means," he whispered finally, "that you are my brother!"

Discipline is not a word we like very much. As children, our parents discipline us to teach us how to behave and be responsible. As adults, God disciplines us for the same reasons. But how can a loving God discipline His children? Shouldn't He be kind to us and give us all we need?

Being kind to a child—or an adult—doesn't mean giving them everything they want and letting them behave however they'd like. What we *need* is to know that following *God's* way is the only *safe* way through this life. Like a parent who spanks a child for running out into the road, God sees the terrible dangers we face, and He knows that if He doesn't discipline us for the small transgressions we make, the big ones might just kill us.

Just as that parent loves the child enough to train him to be safe, God loves *us* enough to do the same.

> My son, do not despise the LORD's discipline and do not resent his rebuke, because the LORD disciplines those he loves, as a father the son he delights in.   PROVERBS 3:11–12

Of course, we always have the choice of simply doing what is right to begin with, so that no "lessons" are necessary!

Lessons

Light two violet candles and the pink candle.

The realization that they were from the same tribe of Judah had kept Jotham and Bartholomew talking late into the night. They were brothers, Jotham had said, because somewhere in their past they shared some great-great-great-grandfather or such. They vowed to always treat each other as brothers should and to pray for each other on all occasions.

"Do you see that strange star?" Bartholomew asked as they stared out the window. "Do you see how it seems to lead in one direction?"

"Yes, I do!" Jotham answered excitedly. "I have been watching it for many nights!"

"Then we will *both* watch that star from now on and pray that Jehovah will use it to guide us back to each other someday!"

Jotham thought this a grand idea, and finally they lay down to sleep.

Bartholomew awakened just before dawn with the rest of the boys. Jotham was still sound asleep. Bartholomew tried kicking his friend lightly several times to wake him, but Jotham only rolled over. Finally Bartholomew whispered, "Jotham, get up!"

The other boys in the dormitory looked crossly at Bartholomew for talking, and he hoped he was not earning another spanking from the Rabbi, but he couldn't let his friend sleep his way into trouble. After all, Andrew had risked such a fate to help *him* on one of his first mornings.

"It is time for morning prayers!" Bartholomew whispered.

Jotham didn't move but from under the blankets said, "I don't feel like going to prayers."

Bartholomew gasped. "You *must* go," he said. "*Every*one must go!"

Still Jotham didn't move, so Bartholomew tried a different tack. Bending down next to Jotham's ear he said in a low voice, "The Rabbi will be most displeased if you do not attend prayers." As he said this he patted Jotham's bottom in a mock spanking. Instantly Jotham's eyes shot open, then his whole body was up and out of bed and dressed.

After morning prayers—during which Bartholomew asked Jehovah to watch after his new friend Jotham—and a breakfast of corn mush—during which Jotham sat with Bartholomew at the head of the table as a Son of David—Jotham helped Bartholomew with his chores. Bartholomew was glad for the help because there were still many urns that had not been moved from the furnace room, since everyone's schedules had been disrupted by Decha.

The sun had moved an hour across the sky when the two boys carried the last of the urns out of the furnace room. They were walking to the scribe's room, with Bartholomew in the lead carrying the top of the urn and Jotham carrying the bottom, when Bartholomew suddenly slipped. The urn went crashing to the ground and broke into thousands of pieces. Just then the Rabbi came walking across the compound and, at the sound of the crash, turned to look. Bartholomew looked back and forth between the urn and the Rabbi, his face looking like that of a cornered rabbit.

"Rr . . . Rabbi . . . ," he stuttered, "forgive me. I slipped in the dirt, and the urn just . . ."

The Rabbi held up his hand to interrupt Bartholomew. He looked slowly from the broken pieces to the panic on the boy's face. "Son of David," he said slowly, "why are you so frightened? Is it because of the lesson you had to learn last night?"

Bartholomew nodded his head. The Rabbi grasped the boy's shoulder and said softly, "Bartholomew, the punishment you received last night was for a willful breaking of our rules. This," he said, sweeping his hand over the shattered urn, "was an accident. We do not punish men *or* boys for making mistakes. Only for acting in disobedience."

Bartholomew stopped quivering and even managed a little smile. Just then Nathan walked up. "Jotham, it is time to leave," he said. Bartholomew and Jotham looked at each other, both knowing they did not want to part but both knowing it had to be if Jotham were ever going to find his family. "Yes, Nathan," Jotham said finally. "I will gather my things."

With Bartholomew's help, Jotham gathered his new clothes, a blanket the dormitory keeper had given him, and a new food bag. Just before they left the dormitory, Bartholomew handed Jotham the walking stick he had been carving. "Here," he said, "I want you to have this. It is my favorite, and it would honor me if you would use it."

Jotham blushed, searching for the right words of thanks. "May your father . . ." he started, then stopped, embarrassed. "May the *God* of your father," he started again, "give you peace and rest in your new home."

As they walked toward the front gate, Bartholomew told Jotham all about Jericho. "I'm sure you will meet Silas," he said. "He is a most wonderful friend and a man of great importance. Yet he will treat you as if *you* are the important one."

"Sounds like Nathan," Jotham said.

"Yes, Silas is very much like Nathan!"

They found the man who had saved them both from the clutches of evil, and Bartholomew asked if he could speak to Nathan before he left.

"Can it not wait until my return?" Nathan asked.

Bartholomew's shoulders fell. "Yes, I suppose it can wait."

Nathan's face changed from impatience to compassion. "Oh, we can spare a minute or two. What is it, boy?"

Bartholomew thought for a moment to put his words in the right order, then said, "I am very confused. Last night the Rabbi spanked me just because I talked during the meal. Then this morning I broke a whole big urn, and he didn't even care. How am I to do right when he is mean and spanks me for no reason, and does not punish me for great wrong?"

Nathan knelt down in the sand next to the boy. "Bartholomew," he said, "did not the Rabbi warn you on many occasions not to talk during meals?" Bartholomew nodded glumly. "And did you obey those warnings?"

"Well," Bartholomew said slowly, dragging it out to give himself time to think. "I *wanted* to obey, and I *tried* to obey, but sometimes I'd just forget. It wasn't my fault."

"Bartholomew," Nathan said patiently, "our actions are our own to choose. I do not remember ever seeing you forget to eat a meal, or go swimming, or carve on that fine walking stick. If you are able to remember to do the things that are important to *you*, then you are able to remember the things that are important to the Rabbi."

"But it is such a foolish rule! Why shouldn't we talk?"

"Foolish or not, it is the rule. And if you want to be a part of this community, you must follow its rules, just as I must follow the rules I do not agree with."

Bartholomew felt as if his insides were going to burst. He knew that Nathan's words were right, but he didn't like it one bit.

"Think of it this way," Nathan said. "You are able to make friends with people you have good reason not to like. Why not try to make friends with the *rules* you do not like?"

"How do you make friends with a *rule*?"

"By making friends with the One who is the Creator of *all* rules and *all* authority, even Caesar himself."

Bartholomew thought about that. "Jehovah?" he asked finally.

"Yes," Nathan answered, "Jehovah. It is an honor to God when we honor those who are in authority over us, even if those authorities rule foolishly or maliciously."

Bartholomew thought he could probably talk about these things for a very long time, but Nathan stood and said it was time for them to leave. Standing by the main gate of Qumran, where men and boys still worked to rebuild the broken-down walls, Bartholomew watched as Nathan once again left him. He waved goodbye to his new friend Jotham.

"Shall I ever see you again?" he said softly to Jotham. Then he added, "Hurry back, Nathan. I shall miss you."

And then he turned to go back to work.

As he carried the heavy urns back and forth, Bartholomew wished he again had the help of his friend Jotham. After work he played Dunk the Donkey with the other boys, then taught Andrew his favorite strategies in King's Ransom. At dinner he kept perfectly quiet throughout the meal and listened closely to the lesson.

The next morning Bartholomew again sat silently through a meal, and he decided if he could do it twice then he could do it always. He noticed that the Rabbi's assistant had returned, and he wondered where he had gone and what he had done. Later Bartholomew was again carrying his urns to the furnace when an alarm went up from the watchtower. "Rider! Coming fast from the north!" the watchman yelled. As always, everyone stopped what he was doing to await word.

"It is a friend," the watchman proclaimed finally, and Bartholomew hoped it was Nathan. "Torkei, from Jericho!"

The name meant nothing to Bartholomew, but all the monks seemed to know who it was and rushed to the gate. A moment later a very tall man riding a very tired horse raced into the compound. The rider dismounted and allowed the horse to guzzle water from a trough. The man was out of breath and gasped great lungfuls of air as he spoke. "I . . . I bring news," he said, pausing to take several more breaths.

Then he looked into the eyes of the monks gathered around him and said five words that stopped Bartholomew's heart as surely as a sword in the chest. "Nathan of Qumran is dead," he said.

And once again, Bartholomew felt as if the whole world had fallen out of the sky.

Sometimes rules don't make any sense—to us! But to those who made the rules, to those in authority over us, the rules are there for very good reasons. Just because we don't understand or like those reasons doesn't mean we can ignore the rules.

Bartholomew hasn't yet figured out *why* it's wrong to talk during meals, but he *has* figured out how to obey the rules. He has finally figured out that by obeying those in authority over him, he's obeying God.

> Everyone must submit himself to the governing authorities, for there is no authority except that which God has established. ROMANS 13:1

Resurrection

Light two violet candles and the pink candle.

The walls of Qumran had probably never heard such crying. From every corner, where a boy would be curled up in a ball, to every doorway, where boys sat with their heads buried in their knees, and every window, behind which boys would try to hide their grief, the sound of wailing echoed off the walls and down the streets of Qumran. It reminded Bartholomew of the night the Romans took over his town, when all the people were gathered in the Court of Elders and cried for the dead.

Every boy in Qumran had been rescued by Nathan, taken in by Nathan, taught by Nathan, loved by Nathan. He was their father.

And now he was dead.

The Rabbi tried to comfort the boys, running from here to there, speaking a few words first to this one, then to that one, then to the one over by the wall. But words did little to comfort, though it was nice he was trying, Bartholomew thought between his own sobs. Words could do little. Only time and Jehovah would heal this wound.

But Bartholomew had an extra reason to cry. Not only was Nathan dead, the messenger had said, but so was his friend Silas. Of the boy Jotham, the messenger did not know. *Two friends dead and one missing*, thought Bartholomew. A tragedy second only to the loss of his parents and siblings.

All work stopped, and the Rabbi declared seven days of mourning, since Nathan was as much loved by the other monks as he was by the boys. Only Nimrod, the Rabbi's assistant, seemed to be unaffected.

The morning sun passed, but no one much noticed. Bartholomew went from Andrew to

Jacob to his other friends, hugging and sobbing and consoling. There was little movement in all of Qumran, every man and boy lost in his own thoughts.

Just before the sun was straight overhead, the watchman in the tower, who was himself grieving loudly, controlled his sobs long enough to yell with a cracked voice, "Riders! Five men coming fast from Jericho!"

Mourning for the dead instantly gave way to survival of the living. Five riders could mean Decha, and that, of course, meant trouble. A moment later, their fears took flesh. Decha of Megiddo, his billowing robes stained with dust and mud and blood, charged into the compound like an army legion attacking a fortress. He slid his horse to a stop and dismounted in one great leap. Eyeing the gathering group of monks, he spotted one and stormed over to him.

To everyone's surprise but Bartholomew's, it was Nimrod, the Rabbi's assistant.

"You told me I'd find Nathan in Jericho," Decha roared, and a gasp of shock shot through the crowd like an arrow. "Now tell me where I can find the boy Jotham!"

Nimrod looked nervously from side to side. "I . . . I told you nothing. You must be thinking of someone else . . ."

Without warning, Decha drew his razor-edged sword and in a flash almost too fast to see, sliced off the end of Nimrod's nose. The cut was so perfectly executed that it didn't do any damage to the nose proper, just the fleshy part at the end. But the result was just as painful, and the Rabbi's assistant grabbed his nose, screaming.

"I have no time for fools or foolish games," he growled. "You sold me the fool Nathan, now sell me the boy or forfeit your life!"

Nimrod was still clutching his nose with both hands and backing away. "I know not where the boy could be!" he cried, though with his nose covered his words sounded more like the quacking of a duck. "I only knew of their plans to travel to Jericho because I overheard them talking on the beach. Where the boy would think to go, I cannot say . . ."

The other monks were in shock to learn that the assistant of their leader had betrayed one of their order. And the Rabbi almost fainted, falling back into the arms of some other monks. The word "Murderer!" was whispered about, as were "Traitor!" and "Thief!"

"Perhaps there are some details you have forgotten," Decha bellowed, sticking Nimrod in the chest with the point of his sword, pushing him farther and farther back into the crowd. "Perhaps you hope to raise the price of the information I seek. Or perhaps you think your half-brother Festavian will save you once again!"

Bartholomew's mouth dropped open. The Rabbi's assistant, brother to the slave owner Festavian of Caesarea? It was almost too big a thought for Bartholomew to think. But then, he realized, it all made sense. How else could two skunk faces be born in the same country?

"No, Decha, I swear!" Nimrod sobbed.

"Monks are not allowed to swear!" Decha replied. "But then, neither are they allowed to sell murder. So why should I think you are not a liar?"

Nimrod was back against a wall now, and the crowd of monks and boys drew in around him such that Bartholomew could no longer see. He could hear, though, and what he heard was Decha yelling, "Tell your lies to me, or tell them to your God!"

"Please, Decha," Bartholomew heard, "I know noth . . ."

There was a short cry, a gasp, then a gurgling sound. The crowd of monks cried out in dismay, and when they backed away Bartholomew saw Decha standing over the dead body of Nimrod. Decha returned his sword to its sheath, then reached into Nimrod's tunic and pulled out a money bag. "Monks were never meant to have blood money," he said to the dead man.

Turning to the rest of Qumran, Decha ordered all boys to be brought to the center of the compound. Bartholomew followed his friends, his knees trembling so badly he thought they would make a fine dance if he weren't so scared. Decha began an inspection of the boys, passing quickly by the tall ones and the short ones and the black ones and the ones that obviously came from Persia. He stopped briefly at this boy and that, all of them fairly close to Jotham's age and size. But when he got to Bartholomew, he stopped for such a long time that Bartholomew was sure the thief would kill him with his stare.

"What's your name, boy?" Decha commanded.

"Bartholomew. Bartholomew of Taricheae."

Decha laughed as a mean boy might laugh when pulling the wings off a fly. "There *is* no more Taricheae," he said.

"I know," Bartholomew replied. "I was there when it was destroyed."

"Then you are not a shepherd boy?"

"No, sir. I am the son of a fisherman."

"And your name is not Jotham?"

"No, sir. It is Bartholomew."

"Then why," Decha said, leaning in close, "do I remember your face so clearly?"

Bartholomew's voice was trembling as much as his knees, and he had to force his answer out through a dry throat and a dry tongue that stuck to the roof of his mouth. "Perhaps you remember me from your earlier visit here," he said. "Remember, 'I have a secret . . . the Messiah is born.'"

Decha stared for another long moment, then leaned in even closer until Bartholomew could smell the stench of his breath and see the bugs crawling in his beard. "I remember," he hissed in Bartholomew's face. "And let me tell you, boy: Your Messiah *was* born. And I killed him!"

Bartholomew didn't react, knowing this to be an empty boast. Then Decha was gone, moving on down the line of boys as his henchmen searched the buildings once again. Finding no boy named Jotham, the thieves gathered again in the compound and Decha spoke to the Rabbi.

"I have not forgotten," he said loud enough to fill the whole village, "that you swore to me you knew of no fool and boy. This man of honor," he continued, pointing his sword at the body of Nimrod, "has told me otherwise. Know this, all of you," he roared even louder, "that I shall return to Qumran as soon as I am done with the boy Jotham. And I will kill any man or boy I find still here!"

The monks gasped once again and immediately started debating the threat. Before Decha had even ridden out of the compound, various plans and theories were being discussed for the survival of the village. The body of Nimrod was quickly spirited away, and another great debate began as to whether he deserved an honorable burial or should simply join the ashes of the garbage heap. It was eventually decided that he deserved the latter.

The shock of learning that Nathan had been killed because of a traitor in their midst only intensified the grief of the Qumran community. Bartholomew said over and over to his friends, "If only I had told Nathan I saw Nimrod acting suspiciously!" and over and over again his friends assured him it would have made no difference.

The seven days of mourning wore on, with only cold meals being served. Many of the monks ripped their tunics off their bodies, then sat in the middle of this or that cold fire pit throwing ashes on their heads.

Bartholomew just moped around the little village, talking quietly with his friends, thinking hard thoughts about his life. He decided to fast in memory of his friend, and so he ate nothing and drank only a bit of water. At night he would stare at the strange star in the sky and wonder if Jotham were still alive to see it as well. "Jehovah," he prayed, "if you can put such a star in the heavens, can you not protect my friend Jotham? Can you not send the Messiah to heal the pain in our hearts?"

By the evening of the fourth night of mourning he had decided that his life could never again be happy in Qumran, and he would leave there to seek a new place to live. He went to the Rabbi's room to tell him this, but the Rabbi was sitting with his head in his arms at his little table, an oil lamp burning overhead. Bartholomew thought the Rabbi was asleep, so he turned to go as quietly as he could. But a creak of his sandal caught the ear of the Rabbi, and the Rabbi looked up.

Bartholomew thought he was looking at the face of death.

The Rabbi's eyes were black and seemed to be set back in his head. The skin of his face was slack, as if all the fat had been sucked out, leaving only the skin. His beard was tangled and caked with dried drool, and his hair hung about his head like greasy rope. The Rabbi squinted at Bartholomew for a long moment, then finally croaked, "Bartholomew." The way he said it was as if he had been searching for the boy's name and then found it, with no interest in that name at all.

"Yes, Rabbi, it is Bartholomew. May I be of some service to you?"

The Rabbi stared for a long time again, then answered in a voice so soft Bartholomew could hardly make out the words. "No, child. There is nothing you can do for me."

The Rabbi said nothing further, and Bartholomew wondered if he should leave. But he knew that something bad was happening here, and only he could stop it.

"I could bring you some tea," Bartholomew offered, but the offer brought no response.

Finally he sat down at the table next to the Rabbi, who continued to stare at the spot where Bartholomew had been standing as if Bartholomew were still standing there. The boy put his hand on the man's arm. "I miss him too," was all Bartholomew could say.

The Rabbi turned his head slowly until he was once again looking into Bartholomew's eyes. "I killed him," he said, and Bartholomew knew exactly how he felt.

"So did I," he said after a moment, and the words were enough of a surprise to bring a bit of life to the Rabbi's eyes.

"No, it was I—," he started to say, but Bartholomew cut him off.

"I saw your assistant ride out after Decha, but I did not tell anyone," he said.

"But it was I who raised Nimrod to the level of assistant, and I who trusted him, even in opposition to the others."

Bartholomew thought about these things for a long time, then said, "Perhaps it is not your fault and it is not my fault. Perhaps," he said quietly, "it was the fault of Nimrod."

The Rabbi turned away, his face reflecting the turmoil of his mind. When he looked back, Bartholomew thought he saw just a bit more life in his eyes. "You are wise beyond your age, Bartholomew," he said. "I have been used and misled by my own folly. Nathan *played* the part of a fool," he said, "but I *am* the fool . . ."

"My father told me that no man is a fool if he follows Jehovah and follows his heart. Have you not done this?"

"A wise father, a wise son. How fortunate I am to have you at Qumran." Then the Rabbi took a deep breath and seemed a little more like his old self. "You need not fear," he said loudly. "You and the other boys may stay here. As long as I am Rabbi, you shall have a home at Qumran! Nathan was right. He was right about you, he was right about many things. If we are to be followers of Jehovah, then we must do Jehovah's work. And if Nathan were standing here, I'd tell him that right to his face!"

"It is good to hear you say that," came a voice from the door. The Rabbi and Bartholomew just about fell off their stools as they turned and saw standing there Nathan of Qumran, filling the door frame and looking very much alive.

Nimrod lived a selfish life, caring only for his own desires.
Nathan lives an *un*selfish life, caring only for the needs of others.
Who would you rather be?

> Do nothing out of selfish ambition or vain conceit, but in humility consider others better than yourselves. Each of you should look not only to your own interests, but also to the interests of others.　　PHILIPPIANS 2:3–4

Special Instructions for Week Four

Because Advent always starts on Sunday but Christmas is on a different day each year, Advent can last anywhere from twenty-one to twenty-eight days. Therefore the last week of *Bartholomew's Passage* is in seven parts. The following table will help you determine which parts to read each day this week, depending on which day Christmas Eve falls. (See the chart on page 173.)

If Christmas Eve is on Sunday or Mon-day, you may want to break up the reading by singing a carol or sharing in some other activity between each part.

Instead of devotional thoughts, each part is followed by a question to consider. Use the question or questions of the day as a discussion starter, or consider them seriously in your own heart. But either way, have a wonderful week: Christmas is coming!

If Christmas Eve is on:

	Sun	Mon	Tues	Wed	Thur	Fri	Sat
Sunday	1–7	1–5	1–3	1–2	1–2	1	1
Monday		6–7	4–5	3–4	3	2	2
Tuesday			6–7	5	4	3	3
Wednesday				6–7	5	4	4
Thursday					6–7	5	5
Friday						6–7	6
Saturday							7

(Read these parts on:)

Bartholomew's Passage

Light the violet candles and the pink candle each day.

Part One

Nathan stood in the doorway. The light from the Rabbi's lamp barely reached that far, leaving Nathan's face clouded in dim shadows, highlighted here and there with a splash of orange light. *Was this a ghost?* Bartholomew wondered. *Or has my fasting made me see things which are not there?*

But then the Rabbi stood slowly, looking like an old man who can no longer make his creaky bones do his bidding. Shuffling across the room, bony hand outstretched, he croaked, "Nathan? Nathan, is that you?"

"Yes, Rabbi," came the soft reply. "It is I."

Bartholomew's mind had frozen, could not think, could not even understand what it was doing. But some part of his mind told his legs to move, and a moment later he had run past the Rabbi and jumped into Nathan's arms. Hugging his friend tighter than he had ever hugged anything, Bartholomew cried a long and happy cry. Nathan didn't say a word but just let the boy release all his tears.

Finally Bartholomew's tears slowed enough and his mind became aware enough to realize that the Rabbi was there as well, one hand on Bartholomew's back, the other on Nathan's shoulder. His cheek, too, was wet with tears.

When Nathan spoke, his voice seemed to Bartholomew to be filled with a weariness he'd never noticed in the man before. Nathan was always so cheerful and happy. Now his voice was filled with great sorrow.

"It is good to be home again," he said at last. "My adventures have not been pleasant, nor is my news at all joyous." At this Bartholomew pulled back and looked his friend in the eye, fearing the worst about Jotham. "Our friend Silas is dead," Nathan said, "killed by Decha."

Bartholomew shuddered a bit and felt a familiar sadness fill his chest, but he had no more tears to cry. Besides, there was a piece of news he was still waiting for. "And our friend Jotham?" he asked, almost too afraid to hear the answer.

At last Nathan smiled a bit. "Jotham is safe and well," he said. Then Nathan sat them down at the Rabbi's table and told them the whole story, how they had arrived at Silas's house, where they met a new friend, Hasrah of Bethlehem; how Silas had taken them all to a meal at an inn; and how, somehow, Decha knew they would be in Jericho and had been waiting for them at the inn. Decha's men had attacked, and Nathan had asked Hasrah to escape with Jotham to the home of Zechariah, a priest living in the hills.

"But Decha found Jotham there and kidnapped him. Zechariah's men tracked them down and killed most of Decha's men, but Decha and two others escaped."

"What about Jotham?" the Rabbi asked.

"Jotham was in fine condition, though his spirit was, of course, upset. But I took him back to Jericho and put him on the caravan of a friend, and he is safely on his way to Jerusalem. My friends will not leave him until they find his family."

When Nathan had finished his story, the Rabbi spoke. "We have news as well," he said. "My assistant, Nimrod, was a traitor. He sold you and the boy to Decha. That's how Decha knew you were in Jericho."

Nathan's mouth dropped open, and for the first time since Bartholomew had met him, his friend didn't know what to say.

"Decha came back here looking for Jotham, and he killed Nimrod," the Rabbi explained.

There was a long silence as Nathan just stared at the Rabbi and thought about his words. Then he said, "It is not your fault, Rabbi," and Bartholomew wondered how Nathan knew what had so vexed the Rabbi.

"I know this in my head," the Rabbi answered, "but my heart does not yet believe it."

Nathan put his hand on the Rabbi's. "Believe it, my friend. I didn't like the man much myself, but I never would have thought him capable of such treachery."

The Rabbi nodded.

The three talked through the night, although Bartholomew must have fallen asleep because when he opened his eyes he found himself lying on the Rabbi's bed, sunlight from the window warming him. As they all walked into the prayer room for morning prayers, the whole of Qumran stared. The boys, not caring at all about the rules, surrounded Nathan and cheered and cried and talked. Finally the Rabbi restored order to the meeting. When he prayed, he thanked Jehovah for the return of Nathan, and prayed for the soul of Silas and for the safety of Jotham's journey. As Bartholomew prayed in his own heart, he prayed that Jotham would find his family, that the Messiah would come soon, and that he would always be able to stay at Qumran with Nathan.

After that, routine was restored to Qumran. The men and boys went back to their jobs and meals were served twice that day. Everything was normal, except that the Rabbi was nowhere to be found. He didn't attend meals, and he sent word that another monk was to lead the prayers. For the whole next day the Rabbi secluded himself in his room, refusing food. At night Bartholomew could see a lamp burning in the Rabbi's window for as late as Bartholomew could stay awake, and he worried that the Rabbi was again feeling guilty about Nimrod.

But the next night, as all the men and boys stood at their places waiting for the evening meal to begin, the door opened and the Rabbi walked in, seeming to Bartholomew a much younger man than he had been two nights before. In the silence that followed the Rabbi walked to the front of the room, to his place at the head table right across from Bartholomew, and stood quietly. Then he lifted his head and prayed, "Jehovah, we thank You for that which You alone have provided. May it strengthen us for Your service."

Everyone said, "Selah," out of habit, then sat down and started passing the food. The Rabbi remained standing, his hands folded behind his back. "In these last days," he said slowly, "I have been thinking much about Qumran."

At that he gave a hard look down the row of boys at the first table, and Bartholomew gulped. "There are going to be some changes around here," the Rabbi continued.

And Bartholomew's heart sank, knowing what was about to happen.

Consider: Nathan lives, but Silas was killed. Is that fair? Why doesn't God just erase all evil from the world?

Part Two

The Rabbi paused, putting his thoughts together, and Bartholomew wished he'd just hurry up and get it over with. "I have prayed to Jehovah for guidance," the Rabbi said finally, "and have sought His will in all things. I have heard Him in my heart," he said, looking into every eye, for the monks had stopped eating to watch him, "and have made some decisions that will affect all of us. First," he continued, with a look at Nathan, "I am appointing Nathan of Hebron as my assistant, to help me guide this flock."

The face of every boy at every table lit up at this news, and they all wanted to cheer but knew better than to make a sound. "And I have decided," the Rabbi continued, "that Qumran is, and shall remain, a refuge for the orphaned sons of Jehovah." At this the boys could no longer contain themselves, and a great cheer went up such as Qumran's walls had never heard. Even the other monks, including the sour-faced Ezra himself, grinned at the news. When the assembly had finally quieted down, the Rabbi went on.

"I am convening a council of the elders," he said, "the newest member of which shall be Nathan, to review the rules in the Manual of Discipline. Qumran is and shall remain a sanctuary for God as well, and we will continue to seek Him and purify ourselves for His service. But we must be sure that the rules of men do not interfere with the work of God, and thus we will challenge any rule that does not further our ability to serve."

The room was quiet as the monks thought about this, but Bartholomew only hoped that meant they could have lunch each day.

"Finally," the Rabbi said, "we will no longer remain isolated behind these walls." At this several of the monks gasped, and Bartholomew could see they were actually afraid of leaving this place. "We shall continue to live most of our days here," the Rabbi said, "and continue to copy the scrolls of the books of God. But under the direction of Nathan, we will on occasion be sending out small groups of men to take those words of Jehovah into all the cities of Palestine." Several of the monks looked at each other, afraid and confused, but most just nodded at the wisdom of the Rabbi's decision.

There was a moment of silence, then, as the Rabbi formed the last of his thoughts into words. "Men of Qumran," he said slowly, then looking at the boys added, "and *young* men of Qumran, it is time for us to stop pretending to be men of God while doing only that which serves ourselves. We must reach beyond these walls, to all the people of Jehovah. The Messiah is coming, men. And *we* must help prepare the way for Him!"

There was another great cheer, louder than the first, followed by excited talking and a hundred predictions about how life in Qumran would change. And it was because of all this noise that no one heard the alarm of the watchman in the tower, nor the pounding of horse hooves in the compound, nor the running feet outside the walls of the dining hall.

But when the door burst open and revealed a strange sight, every man and boy of Qumran was instantly silent. The man wore the colorful robes and turban of a Persian trader, though he was covered from head to toe with the dust of the road. He was breathing great gulps of air, and sweat from his scalp made mud of the dust on his face. Looking over the group like a wild man looking for an escape, he yelled out, "Nathan of Qumran! I seek Nathan of Qumran!"

Some of the monks thought the man crazed and stood to protect Nathan. But Nathan himself stood slowly and walked over to the man. "I am Nathan," he said.

"I am sent by Salamar of Persia," he said, "and I bring you news. The boy Jotham has been lost!"

Consider: We need to have rules and traditions in our society, but how did some of Qumran's rules prevent them from doing God's will? Do *we* have any rules and traditions like that in *our* churches?

Part Three

Nathan was in his bedchamber hastily repacking his travel bag as Bartholomew looked on. Fool's cap, old ragged tunic, prayer shawl, water skin . . . The Rabbi spoke as Nathan packed.

"What do you think happened to the boy?" he asked.

"I do not know, Rabbi," Nathan said quickly, "but I smell Decha of Megiddo in this!"

"Where will you begin your search?"

Nathan stopped for a moment, thinking. "I believe I will head straight for Jerusalem and work back from there. Salamar and his men are searching the desert from their camp toward Jerusalem. We should meet in the middle and hopefully find Jotham."

"And if you find Decha instead? What will you do?"

Nathan sighed. "I do not know, Rabbi. But I know that I will give my life to keep Jotham out of Decha's hands!"

As Nathan resumed packing, the Rabbi excused himself. Bartholomew was deep in thought. The messenger had said that Jotham had been playing with a kite in the desert and then just disappeared. They had begun a search, but Salamar, leader of the caravan and Nathan's friend, knew that Nathan would want to know of the event.

The Rabbi returned a few moments later, a long, curved sword held gently in his hands. "I would like you to take this, Nathan," he said.

Nathan stopped packing and pulled back from the sword as if it were a snake. "Rabbi, I have not used a sword since I was twenty years old," he said slowly. "And you know what tragedies *that* brought!"

The Rabbi nodded. "Yes, yes, I know. And I, too, have lived most my life free of violence. It is a most distasteful thing. Our trust is in Jehovah alone to protect us. But I am beginning to think that sometimes Jehovah needs a little help! So, please take this, Nathan. Protect yourself. Protect the boy."

Nathan thought about this for several heartbeats, then put his hand on the Rabbi's shoulder and said, "I am often tempted to pick up a sword when I see how the Romans treat us. But it has not been my way for a very long time, Rabbi. God has always kept His hand on my travels. I dare not start depending on my *own* strength now."

The Rabbi nodded and propped the sword against the wall. Bartholomew had been watching all this, thinking about all these things, and finally he could contain himself no longer. "Nathan, may I go with you?" he asked.

Nathan shook his head slowly. "No, child. This journey will be full of danger. I cannot allow it."

"But *all* my journeys have been full of danger! And Jehovah has kept me safe, has He not?"

"Yes, but this is different."

"It is different only because this time it is I who will be helping another, instead of another helping me!"

"Exactly," Nathan said. "You have had all your adventures because you had no choice. Someone else was forcing you into it. But to *choose* danger is a matter for adults. You are not yet old enough to make that decision."

"I know," Bartholomew said, which surprised Nathan. "That's why I'm asking you to make it for me. I will not disobey you, Nathan. Jotham told me what terrible tragedies that can cause. But I will *beg* you to allow me to help search for my friend."

Nathan hesitated, so Bartholomew plunged ahead. "I know I am small," he pleaded, "but my eyes are young and strong. I can make friends with *any*one and get them to help us or feed us or do anything else we need. I can run messages for you, or cook for you, or . . . or . . . or even wash your tunic. But I will not slow you down or be in your way. *Please*, Nathan. I cannot stand the thought of sitting here doing nothing when my friend Jotham is in trouble!"

Nathan sighed a long sigh, then looked to the Rabbi. "What do you think, Rabbi?" he asked.

The Rabbi frowned deeply and shook his head. "The boy is a troublemaker and a pest. He cannot follow instructions and is clumsy as an ox. If you would get him out from under my feet, I would be most grateful."

Bartholomew was shocked at the harsh words, but the Rabbi smiled. Bartholomew looked quickly to Nathan.

Nathan sighed again. "Very well," he said. "I shall take him with me and relieve you of your burden."

Bartholomew hesitated, looking from face to face, not sure he had understood correctly. But then both the men let out loud laughs, and Bartholomew knew they were joking with him, and that he really was being allowed to go with Nathan. He could feel his insides light up like the special star he had seen.

"Go quickly and pack," Nathan said to the boy, and before the last of the cook fires had been put out for the night, Nathan and Bartholomew walked out of Qumran and into the dark with the prayers and blessings of the whole community.

Consider: Bartholomew learned the lesson of obedience well and so submitted himself to the authority of Nathan. Does it ever turn out good for us when we disobey those in authority over us?

Part Four

The moon was bright as the two travelers climbed the hills above the Sea of Death. The trail was rough, but Bartholomew had no trouble keeping up. *In fact,* he thought, *I could go a lot faster if I didn't have to keep waiting for Nathan.*

Through the long hours of the night they walked, stopping only once for a bite of the food John the cook had packed for them. Bartholomew didn't know how far they had traveled, or how far they had yet to go, but just before he thought the sky should begin to brighten with the pink of morning, they came across a stand of buildings poking up out of the desert. Nathan went to the door of a house and rapped his knuckles on the door.

There was some mumbling inside, and some banging around, then finally a voice called through the wood slats. "Who is that?" the voice demanded. "Who is there?"

"Nathan of Qumran. And if you don't open this door and let me in, I shall tell the whole world how you *really* caught that fish that day!"

Instantly the door swung open and there, an oil lamp in his hand illuminating his face, stood the oldest man Bartholomew had ever seen. "Come in, my friend," the man said with a grin, "and keep your tales to yourself."

They entered the little house and saw an old woman, who had obviously just gotten out of bed herself. "Nathan!" she called, and gave him a kiss on the cheek. "How is it we see you again so soon?"

"Jotham has been lost," was all Nathan said.

"Again!" the old woman cried.

Concern clouded the old man's face. "Decha?" he asked.

"I do not know. We know only that he is lost." Then turning to Bartholomew he said, "Bartholomew, these are my friends, the priest Zechariah and his wife, Elizabeth." To the old couple he said, "This is Bartholomew, friend of Jotham."

"Then a friend of ours as well," said Zechariah, and Bartholomew decided he liked these people already. A baby started crying. Bartholomew didn't see where his mother was, so he asked.

"Elizabeth is the baby's mother," Nathan said. And then he explained how the baby was named John, and he was a cousin of Jotham. "He is a special baby," Elizabeth said, and Zechariah told Bartholomew a long story about faith and the miracles of God. When they had finished, Bartholomew sat for several minutes as his thoughts found order. "If John is here to prepare the way of the Messiah," he asked finally, "then doesn't that mean the Messiah Himself must soon be born?"

The adults looked at each other and smiled. "You have brought a very wise young man with you," Zechariah said to Nathan. To Bartholomew he said, "Yes, it means that exactly. The Messiah *shall* soon be born, and in fact, we have met His mother."

Bartholomew's jaw dropped open. "Who?" he wheezed. "Who is the mother of the Messiah?"

"My cousin Mary," Elizabeth said. "She is even now great with child, though she has been with no man." Bartholomew thought for another few moments, then Elizabeth said, "Now you must rest. And when you awake, I shall have a fine breakfast for you."

The two weary travelers gladly lay down for a few hours of sleep, though sleep was long in coming for Bartholomew as he thought about the Messiah. When he awoke, sunshine filled the house with light as Elizabeth's cooking filled it with a smell so wonderful Bartholomew was sure he had found heaven. "This is parched wheat," Elizabeth told him as she dished some onto a plate. Bartholomew wondered why parched wheat would look so much like corn but didn't ask. "It was Jotham's favorite while he stayed with us," the old woman added.

After breakfast and prayers, Nathan and Bartholomew waved goodbye to the old couple. Many questions were on Bartholomew's mind, but he decided to wait until they weren't in such a hurry before asking them.

Nathan and Bartholomew climbed through hills so rough and craggy that Bartholomew thought they would surely cut a man in half should he slip. "Isn't there a *road* to Jerusalem?" he asked at one point.

"Yes, there is," Nathan answered, huffing and puffing. "The Romans have built many fine roads. But none take such a direct route to Jerusalem as this path. We can make the journey much more quickly this way." Then he added, "That is also why I turned down Zechariah's offer of a donkey. A beast of burden would only slow us down."

It was long after their noon meal, and the sun was low in the sky, when Nathan and Bartholomew crested a high, round hill. Below the hill was a valley so green that it reminded Bartholomew of Taricheae, and on the hill across the valley sat a city that glowed like diamonds in the setting sun. It was surrounded by a high wall, and everywhere towers and domes pushed their way into the sky.

"Welcome to Jerusalem," Nathan said, breathing hard. And Bartholomew instantly thought of all the friends he could make in such a place.

Consider: Everywhere Bartholomew goes he is anxious to hear and learn about God. How might God bless us if we have such zeal for Him?

Part Five

Glad to have reached their destination, the two friends trekked down the hill into the valley, sloshed across a cool stream, lapping up some of its waters, then started up the hill toward the city wall. Many shepherds and caravans were camped in the valley, and a moment later Nathan stopped short and pointed to one.

"If I'm not mistaken . . . ," he said. Then without another word he marched over to a caravan surrounded by tents so colorful that they looked like a field of flowers. Nathan searched among the caravan, then finally spotted a large, dark-skinned man.

"Salamar!" he cried, and the man turned toward them. His face lit up, and he met his old friend with a bear hug. "It is good to see you again, Nathan," he said. "And I have good news for you. Jotham of Jericho has been found!"

"Praise be to Jehovah!" Nathan said, and Bartholomew felt a large weight lift off his own chest. "How did this occur?"

"The boy and my son were chased into a tunnel by one called Decha of Megiddo." At this Nathan's face grew angry.

"I should have accepted the Rabbi's sword!" he said. "That thief has been trouble for too long!" Then, turning back to Salamar, he asked, "But how did you end up in Jerusalem?"

"The tunnel led to some catacombs," Salamar answered, "and the catacombs led here, to Jerusalem. A man named Simeon helped the boys escape Decha's hands."

Bartholomew had been silent for as long as he could. "And what of Ishtar?" he asked. "Is your son Ishtar safe?"

Nathan looked at the boy, shocked that he knew the name of Salamar's son. But then a curious look crossed Salamar's face, and a moment later he said, "Bartholomew? Bartholomew of Taricheae, is that you?"

"Yes," the boy answered.

Salamar dropped to one knee and hugged the boy tightly. "It is good to see you. But how is it you end up in Jerusalem with this old troublemaker, Nathan?"

Bartholomew quickly explained all that had happened to him, and Salamar was genuinely sad at the boy's story. Nathan looked on, quite perplexed, and finally Salamar turned to him and explained.

"We were camped on the shores of Galilee near Taricheae," he said. "Bartholomew came over and made friends with us, and he traded me the finest of redfish I have ever tasted for a bit of tea!" Turning back to Bartholomew he asked, "Did you make good use of the tea?"

"Oh, yes," Bartholomew answered quickly. "I traded it for a fine ram's horn!"

Nathan just shook his head in wonder, then asked, "Where is Jotham now? May we see him?"

Salamar shook his head. "No, he is not here. He was searching Jerusalem for his family when some old prophetess told him to look in Bethlehem. Simeon seemed quite taken by the woman's words and escorted Jotham there this afternoon."

Bartholomew's heart saddened again that he could not see his friend. "How far is it to Bethlehem?" he asked Nathan.

"Only two hours' walk."

Bartholomew looked at the sun. There was only an hour of daylight left. Nathan saw his disappointment and added, "Perhaps tomorrow we can go there for a visit."

Bartholomew grinned, and just then a dark-skinned boy ran into the compound. "Ishtar!" Bartholomew called out. "It is I, Bartholomew of Taricheae!"

There was a great reunion between the friends, then Bartholomew said to Salamar, "I have seen the strange star you searched for! Did you find it yourself?"

Salamar nodded. "Yes. Jotham showed it to us two nights ago, and it led us in the direction of Jerusalem. But since Jotham has been missing, it has not again appeared."

"But we met your king, Herod," Ishtar said excitedly. "He was most anxious to worship your Messiah when He is born. Father promised to tell him when we find the child!"

Bartholomew seemed to know everything that was going on, and Nathan knew *nothing* of what was going on, so Salamar sat him down to explain. As he did, Bartholomew and Ishtar ran off to renew their friendship.

Later that evening, after a fine meal of celebration, Bartholomew and Ishtar lay talking on their mats outside Ishtar's tent.

"What do you think this new Messiah will be like?" Ishtar asked.

Bartholomew thought a long thought. "I think He will be much like Nathan," he said finally. "Nathan will give up anything to help anyone and never ask anything for himself. And I think that's what the Messiah will be like."

They talked for a long time, mostly about Jotham and the good friend that he was, and were just about ready to lie down to sleep when a bright light from the center of the camp lit up the sky.

"What is *that*?" Ishtar yelled.

"I do not *know*," Bartholomew answered. "Perhaps a tent is on fire!"

The boys looked around, but nothing moved anywhere in the camp. No one else seemed to have noticed, or they were all asleep. Bartholomew jumped up. "Come on!"

Ishtar looked distressed. "We cannot! I am forbidden to leave my tent once my father puts me to bed!"

Bartholomew looked at Ishtar with disgust. "We *must* go look at this thing! Your father would surely understand!"

Ishtar humphed and shook his head. "You are just like Jotham!" he said. But he got up out of his bed and followed Bartholomew through the little village of tents. Not far away, as they rounded the tent of the harem of Ishtar's uncle, they saw the source of the light. Salamar's tent sat in the exact center of the camp and was made of the same light and shiny material as all the other tents. But now it glowed like a bonfire and puffed outward, as if some great wind were blowing. But the air was still, and the tent did not burn, so the two boys were completely curious. Slowly they moved forward, wanting neither to be caught out of bed nor to interrupt some feast that was only for adults. But the light was so brilliant, and the air so full of a sweet scent like honeysuckle, that the boys could not hold themselves back.

Stepping lightly, they slowly moved toward Salamar's tent. Reaching out as carefully as if he were reaching for a snake, Ishtar grabbed the edge of the tent flap between two fingers and slowly pulled it back.

What they saw made both boys gasp. Salamar was turned away from them, lying facedown flat on the floor. And on the other side of him was an angel, its wings moving slowly, shining as brightly as the sun, and speaking words such as the boys had never before heard.

Consider: Are there really such things as angels, waiting to protect and guide us?

Part Six

The light radiating from the angel shimmered like the waves of heat above a fire. *It's like looking at all the gold and diamonds in the world,* Bartholomew thought, *only much more beautiful.* The brightness of the light did not hurt his eyes, but somehow the sight was so . . . so holy that he could not bear to look at it. He covered his face with his fingers and fell to the ground as the angel spoke.

"And so Jehovah has sent me with this message for you, Salamar of Persia," he said, and Bartholomew could hear Ishtar gasp. "Do not trust the king called Herod, for he is not the true King of the Jews. Follow the star, and when you have found the babe, worship Him in secret. For the forces of Herod are cruel and mighty. But the kingdom of God awaits him who obeys. Glory to God in the highest!" the angel boomed out, and the sound rattled the ground. "And on earth, peace, for this is the night of the Messiah's birth!"

Suddenly the tent was dark again. Slowly, Bartholomew raised his head, as did Ishtar and Salamar. The angel was gone, and Bartholomew examined his hands, almost expecting to be burned as if from the sun. So shocked were the boys that neither could say a word. They just looked dumbly from each other to the front of the tent, where the angel had stood, and back again. Salamar, too, sat in shock, until he slowly turned around at the sound of the boys' shuffling.

"Ishtar," he wheezed, "did you see this thing? Did you hear?"

"Yes, Father," Ishtar answered weakly.

"Then go and wake my brothers," the father continued, regaining his composure. "Tell them we must leave at once!"

Soon the whole camp was awake and chattering as Nathan, Salamar, and Ishtar's two uncles consulted. Finally Salamar turned and addressed the whole camp.

"We have decided that the caravan shall remain here," he said loudly enough to be heard, but not so loud his voice would carry to the other camps or inside the wall. "If the entire caravan leaves, Herod will be alerted and send spies. My brothers and I and a dozen men will follow the star when it appears," he said. "We shall take only a few tents and enough food for a day. Nathan, my son, and the boy Bartholomew will accompany us."

Bartholomew and Ishtar grinned at each other.

"I believe I know where the star will lead you, my friend," Nathan said to Salamar. "If you like, we could start in that direction."

Salamar considered this idea. "No, my friend," he said, "we will wait for the star. Perhaps you do know where this Messiah will be born. But we must find Him in our own way."

Nathan smiled and nodded understanding. Suddenly someone shouted, and everyone looked to the sky. "The star!" Bartholomew exclaimed. "That's the same star I saw from Qumran!"

Quickly a few tents were taken down and packed onto camels, along with other provisions. Then the small band started out, following the star up the Kidron Valley and toward the east. The road was flat and paved, unlike the other roads Bartholomew had traveled.

"Jotham said that the Messiah is coming for all people, not just you Jews," Ishtar said as he walked beside Bartholomew.

"It is as Nathan has told us," Bartholomew answered.

Ishtar was silent for a long moment. "I believe I will like having only one God," he said finally. "Perhaps He will answer more prayers than our other gods do."

As all the excitement of seeing the angel and of the hasty departure passed, Bartholomew began to feel sleepy. His head kept nodding as he walked, and he felt as if a soft pillow were stuffed inside his skull. Ishtar, too, kept stumbling beside him, and Bartholomew wondered if there weren't a camel somewhere they could ride.

But then the line came to a sudden stop, and the boys were instantly awake again. Running to the front of the little caravan, they found Salamar and the other men staring into the sky.

"What is it, Father?" Ishtar asked.

"The star," the older man answered. "It has disappeared again."

Both boys searched the sky with the men, but the special star was nowhere to be seen. Then someone yelled, "Look!" and all eyes turned to a little hill across a valley to their right. There, in the dark, sat a small village, covering the top of the hill like a turban on a head.

"Bethlehem," Nathan said, and Bartholomew looked at him in surprise.

"A quiet town," Salamar commented. Then with a sigh he said, "We shall camp here, alongside the road, until the star again appears."

"I believe the star was leading you to that town," Nathan said to his friend. Salamar just shrugged.

"Perhaps," he replied. "But until it guides us directly into the village, or wherever it is taking us, we shall camp here."

As the tents were unloaded and raised, Bartholomew found Nathan and pulled him aside. "That's *Bethlehem!*" he whispered. "Did you not say the Messiah will be born in Bethlehem?"

"Indeed," Nathan whispered back, "it is most definitely so. But Salamar neither knows nor understands the Torah. He knows only the stars and will follow only them."

"But the *Messiah!*" Bartholomew pleaded. "He might even now be born over there!"

"Yes, yes, I know," Nathan said, "but I cannot leave my friend. It would be a terrible insult if it appeared I did not respect his decision." Nathan thought for a moment, then said, "Come with me!"

Together with Ishtar, they found Salamar waiting for his tent to be erected. "Salamar, my friend," Nathan said with a smile, "I believe I shall send Bartholomew into Bethlehem to fetch me some fresh dates. May I send your son Ishtar with him?"

"Dates, at this time of night?" Salamar said.

"For the peace of my inner workings," Nathan said. "My body is objecting to the trek my soul has taken it on."

With a wave of his hand Salamar said, "Oh, that! We have some fine potions that will ease your pain. Some crushed water lily perhaps, or roasted locusts."

Nathan shook his head, "No, no," he said, "those things are strangers to my body. I must have some fresh dates."

Salamar sighed. "Very well. My son may accompany your charge."

"Thank you, my friend," Nathan replied. Then he turned to Bartholomew and handed him some money, saying, "Be sure to hurry back if you find that which you seek!"

Bartholomew understood the hidden meaning and nodded. Then he and Ishtar ran out of the camp and across the valley toward Bethlehem, both wondering if they would find their friend Jotham.

There were many shepherds camped outside the town, and the two boys had to weave their way around goatskin tents and corrals of sheep. Finally they climbed up the other side of the valley and onto the road just where it entered Bethlehem. As they walked into the little town, they passed a man leading a donkey. On the donkey sat a young woman weeping softly. Bartholomew could tell the woman was going to have a baby, and he thought she looked large enough to have twins. The couple passed by, but Bartholomew could not ignore such a situation.

"Good sir," he called to the man, "may I be of service? Your wife weeps, and it is many hours until morning. Is there a need I can meet for you?"

The man stopped walking and turned back to the boys. "I fear not," he said. "My wife is in the pains of childbirth, but I can find no place for her to lay her head. I have been turned away from every inn in Bethlehem."

Bartholomew thought for a moment. "Surely there is at least *one* bed in all of Bethlehem! Would you follow me so I may search for you?"

The man hesitated, then his wife let out a little cry, and he said to Bartholomew, "Yes, yes, we shall try again!"

Bartholomew led the way into the town, walking down the empty streets, past dark and closed-up buildings. He turned down one side street, and then another, searching this way and that. Finally he spied what he was looking for. As the man, the woman, the donkey, and Ishtar waited, Bartholomew went up to the wooden door of an inn and knocked.

There was no reply.

He knocked again, a bit louder, then heard some mumbling from inside. He knocked once more, and there was louder mumbling, followed by bumping noises and a crashing sound. Then the door opened a bit and the hand of a sleeping man fell into the opening down at the floor. The face of another man, the one who had opened the door, appeared in the crack above and said angrily, "What is it?"

Bartholomew was ready and spoke as excitedly as if he were watching a camel race. "Good sir!" he said breathlessly, "what would you say if I told you your stable is on fire!"

The round and bearded face came alive in shock. "My stable! On fire? Call my neighbors! Raise the alarm!"

The man was trying to push the sleeping man out of the door so he could open it as Bartholomew said, "Wait! Wait! I have for you the best of news! Your barn is *not* on fire and instead holds its animals safely!"

The man stopped and stared at Bartholomew, head twisted to one side, confused.

"Now surely," Bartholomew continued, "you will want to reward one who brings you such glorious news!"

The face of the man melted into anger. "So, you would play me the fool!" he shouted, and from somewhere inside the inn someone grumbled, "Quiet!" Lowering his voice, the innkeeper said, "I shall give you nothing, boy, not one shekel!"

"I seek not shekels," Bartholomew said quickly, "nor anything at all for myself. I ask only that you be my friend, and as a friend do me one favor."

The man softened a bit but was still suspicious. "And what sort of favor does a boy ask in the middle of the night?"

"My friends here," Bartholomew answered, turning to the couple with the donkey. "They are in great need of a place to stay and a place to give birth to their child. Could you not spare a room for such needful people?"

"Them!" the man shouted. "I already sent them away! I have no room! My inn is full beyond full!" he said, and he pointed at the sleeping arm at his feet. "I would help them if I could, but there is simply nowhere to put them!"

"Well . . . ," Bartholomew said slowly, "if your stable is not burning, could they not sleep there?"

The man harrumphed and looked away, seemingly trying to think of a reason to refuse the boy. Bartholomew found his best innocent-boy-pleading voice and said, "Surely it is not too much to ask, especially for one who brings you the good news that your stable is not on fire!"

The man laughed despite himself. "No," he said, "it is not too much to ask, especially for a new friend. My name is Hasrah," he said, putting out his hand.

"And I am Bartholomew of Taricheae. May Jehovah grant us a friendship that lasts longer than either of us live!"

"Selah!" said Hasrah, then he added, "I shall fetch some help and clean out the stable."

"Then I will leave these fine people with you," Bartholomew answered, "as I go my way to complete my own journey."

Bartholomew explained what was happening to the man and woman, and the man thanked him greatly, amazed that a ten-year-old boy could accomplish what he could not. With Ishtar by his side Bartholomew headed down the street, and just before they turned out of sight they heard Hasrah open the door again and say to some unseen helper, "We need some fresh hay for our guests to lie on. Go to the meadow . . ."

That was all Bartholomew heard as he turned the corner and set out to search for the Messiah.

Consider: God sent an angel to warn Salamar about Herod. Does He ever give *us* warnings of dangers ahead? What do I have to do to be ready to hear those warnings?

Part Seven

Perhaps we should look in a temple," Ishtar suggested. "That would seem a most likely place for a god to be born."

"I don't think they *have* a temple," Bartholomew said. "The town is too small."

"Well, then, where *will* we look?"

"Nathan said it could be anywhere. We will just have to go from house to house listening for the crying of a baby."

"There must be *many* babies here," Ishtar said. "How will we know which one?"

"Oh, I will know the Messiah when I hear Him," Bartholomew said. "All I have to do is hear His cry or see His mother and father, and I will know. Such a holy thing cannot be hidden!"

The boys walked up and down the streets of Bethlehem, craning their necks this way and that to listen for the cries of babies. They heard one, down a little side street, and saw through a window a mother walking her baby by lamplight. "That is not Him," Bartholomew said quickly. "That is not the mother of a Messiah. I can tell such things. The moment I see her I will know she is the one," he said confidently.

For several minutes they searched, finally reaching the edge of the town, where the shepherds were camped. Bartholomew saw several standing around a fire near a tall tree, then froze in fear. "Ishtar!" he hissed. "We must leave this place!"

Ishtar started to protest, but Bartholomew clamped his hand over his friend's mouth. "That man is Decha of Megiddo!" he whispered.

Ishtar pulled Bartholomew's hand away and whispered, "The man who hunts Jotham?"

"Yes! We must go and get help!"

Running through the dark town, the sound of their sandals echoing off the walls, the two boys raced back to the caravan of Salamar.

"Nathan!" Bartholomew cried. "Nathan! Come quickly!"

Nathan was sitting across a fire from Salamar as the dark-skinned man searched the sky. "What is it?" he called.

"Decha of Megiddo camps outside Bethlehem! His band is awake and surely plots evil!"

At the name of Decha, Nathan jumped up and spun around to look out across the valley toward Bethlehem. "Where?"

Bartholomew searched the darkness, then pointed in the moonlight and said, "There! By that tall tree!"

Nathan looked back at Salamar. "This is a thing I must do," he said. "You must remain here and follow the path Jehovah has set for you. I must go alone to meet Decha."

Salamar looked sad but nodded his head.

"No!" Bartholomew screamed. "We must *all* go! We must fight this thief and kill him!"

Nathan held Bartholomew firmly by the shoulders. "No, child. This is the work of a man. And a fool. The fight I must now fight is mine alone. It is why," he said, looking again at the valley, "Jehovah has brought me to this place."

Bartholomew was crying now, fear of losing his new father overwhelming him. "Please do not go!" he cried. Then he turned to Salamar. "Please, Salamar! Go with him!"

Salamar shook his head sadly again. "Nathan is right, Bartholomew. I have traveled many months to be in this place at this time, following the will of your God. I must believe that He is in control, and each of us must play his own part in this drama."

Just then the faint cries of "Father! Father!" were heard, echoing up from the valley. Everyone looked to see a small boy, about the size of Bartholomew, running across the fields toward a man who was yelling, "Jotham!" Bartholomew could not believe that he was witnessing the reunion of Jotham and his father.

But neither could he believe it when, a moment later, a dark form swept out of the shadows and came between father and son. Two other men captured the father, and, within seconds, they were holding him captive with ropes tied to his wrists.

"Decha!" Nathan spat. Then, turning to the rest of the group, he said, "I must go!"

Salamar held Bartholomew tightly as Nathan raced down the hill. Bartholomew was still crying and fought Salamar's grip. But the Persian leader was much stronger, and he held the boy, both to keep him from running and to hug him close as they watched.

Frustration clamped around Bartholomew's chest like a bony hand. He felt completely helpless as he saw Decha take a huge swing of his sword, aiming right for the neck of Jotham's father.

Just then Nathan came cartwheeling out of the woods and landed between Decha and his target. Bartholomew could not hear what was happening, but he watched as Nathan flipped and slid and twirled around in his best fool's act. Finally Nathan landed right in front of Decha, plucked the sword from the surprised thief's hands, and spun away to safety.

"There!" Bartholomew cried, tugging at Salamar's arms. "Nathan has won. Now may I please go to my friend Jotham?"

Salamar hesitated but then said, "Very well. It seems Nathan has indeed taken control."

Free now, Bartholomew jumped over the side of the road and slid his way down the hill. As he reached the bottom he looked in time to see a rope fly out of the woods behind Nathan. The noose on the rope landed cleanly around Nathan's neck and was then pulled tight by a fat old woman on a broken-down donkey. The woman cackled, and Bartholomew saw that her teeth were black with rot. He recognized her as the woman at the end of Decha's caravan.

Decha swooped over to Nathan and recovered his sword, then once again threatened the neck of Jotham's father. Bartholomew could not hear the words being spoken, but he knew there was much hate in what was being said. Finally Decha again took aim at Jotham's father. Bartholomew ran toward them, not knowing what he would do but knowing he had to do something. Then he heard Nathan yell the name "David!" to Jotham. Bartholomew was completely confused by this but kept running.

As he ran, Bartholomew watched Jotham scoop something up off the ground. Then, like David confronting the giant Goliath, Jotham was swinging something over his head and yelling out the name of Decha. Decha was just bringing his sword up and looked back toward the boy. At that moment Jotham let loose the strip of leather in his hand, and Bartholomew saw a stone the size of an apple fly toward Decha. Decha looked shocked, and then the stone struck him right between the eyes.

And Decha fell dead.

Bartholomew skidded to a stop, breathing hard. Nathan and some other men chased

Decha's two henchmen and the fat old woman, and Bartholomew watched as Jotham and his father ran toward each other across the field.

But then Bartholomew saw something else.

Running down the hill to his left, Bartholomew saw the last one of Decha's men coming from where he'd been holding the horses. In his right arm the man carried a long, pointed lance, such as Roman soldiers use. And he was headed straight for Jotham.

Without even thinking, Bartholomew started down the hill to intercept the thief. "Lion!" he yelled, hoping to distract the man. "There's a lion chasing you!"

But the man didn't pay any attention to the small boy running his way, didn't even bother looking behind him. There was nothing Bartholomew could do to stop him.

"Jotham, look out!" Bartholomew yelled, but with all the commotion in the field, his friend could not hear, and neither he nor his father noticed the approaching danger.

Decha's henchman was closing in on Jotham now. Bartholomew calculated he would break through the trees and skewer Jotham before anyone else could react. Desperate to save his friend, he poured all his strength into his legs. It would be close, and he drove his legs even harder. Thirty feet, twenty, ten . . .

Suddenly the henchman looked toward Bartholomew and laughed. The small boy was no more threat than a mosquito on an elephant. As if to emphasize this, he now put both his hands on the lance, preparing to strike. Bartholomew also knew he was too small to tackle the man or even trip him. So another plan quickly formed inside his head.

Running his hardest, coming in from the henchman's right, he closed the gap between the henchman and himself. Five feet . . . three feet . . . now! With all that was left of his strength, Bartholomew launched himself into the air. But instead of aiming for the thief, he aimed for the front of the thief's lance. He hit it perfectly and wrapped his arms around the heavy shaft.

The henchman wasn't ready for this move and didn't have time to reposition his hands to hold up the added weight. Bartholomew's weight drove the tip of the lance deep into the ground, with Bartholomew still holding tightly to the shaft. The resistance of the ground brought the lance to a sudden stop, but the henchman kept going. Flying head over heels, he was carried up and over Bartholomew by the spring of the lance. His grip on the weapon finally broke, and he did three somersaults through the air before smacking headfirst into a tree.

Bartholomew fell back, gasping for breath, not believing what he'd just done.

Moments later Nathan and two other men ran up, breathing hard. Nathan looked over the scene. Seeing that the henchman had been knocked out, he said, "Well, Bartholomew. It seems as if you have captured the last of Decha's gang!"

The other two men tied up the henchman and led him away. Brushing himself off, Nathan said, "Come, my son, let us return to Salamar."

"But, *Nathan!*" Bartholomew exclaimed. "I want to go see Jotham!"

Nathan shook his head. "No, boy, not just yet. Jotham will be here in the morning. For now, we must leave him to rejoice with his parents."

Which was, Bartholomew saw, exactly what was happening. Through the trees he saw Jotham hugging his father. Then a woman came screaming out of a tent and scooped Jotham up in her arms. Tears formed in Bartholomew's eyes, tears of happiness for his friend and tears of sadness that he would never have such a reunion himself.

Nathan and Bartholomew reached the top of the hill, and Salamar greeted them warmly. This adventure would be written down for all to read, he proclaimed, and a great feast of celebration would be set for Jotham and his family. But just as these plans were being made, and just as Bartholomew was beginning to wonder again about the Messiah, a light appeared in the sky above the valley. And for the second time that night, Bartholomew thought he had never seen a sight so holy.

Consider: Jesus was born into a dark world, a world of cruelty and death. What was it about Him that made Him a *light* to the world?

Beginnings and Endings

Light all of the candles.

Bartholomew shielded his eyes and looked up. In the field below women screamed and men drew their swords. The light spread out until it seemed to cover the entire sky, and Bartholomew fell on his face, afraid to look. Then a voice, loud and deep, came booming from above.

"Do not be afraid," the voice said, "I bring you good news of great joy that will be for all the people." At these words the screaming in the valley stopped. Bartholomew dared to take a peek through his fingers and saw that the men below had lowered their swords. Every ear listened as they gazed at the glowing form above them, no longer needing to shield their eyes. The form was that of a dark-skinned man with long, flowing hair. He was dressed in white robes with blue and purple sashes. He hovered in the air, light shining from his very being. He held a trumpet in his right hand and a golden scepter in his left.

"Today in the town of David," the angel continued, "a Savior has been born to you; he is Christ the Lord. This will be a sign to you: You will find a baby wrapped in cloths and lying in a manger."

Suddenly from nowhere there appeared thousands of angels, some near, some far. They covered the sky as far as Bartholomew could see, and lit up the world with their glow. And every single one of them seemed to be looking directly at Bartholomew.

As they appeared, the angels began to sing "Glory to God," and it was the most beautiful sound Bartholomew had ever heard. "Glory to God in the highest, and on earth peace to men on whom his favor rests!"

Over and over the angels sang, "Glory to God in the highest." So holy was the sight that Bartholomew hid his face in his arms once again, not daring to look any longer at the angelic beings.

And then, quite suddenly, it was quiet.

Bartholomew looked up and saw that the sky was once again dark. He stood up slowly, as did Nathan beside him.

"The Messiah has been born," Nathan whispered.

Bartholomew looked at him, then back to the sky, the words of the angel spinning through his head. "This will be a sign to you," he muttered under his breath. "You will find a baby wrapped in cloths and lying in a . . ."

Bartholomew whipped around and looked Nathan square in the eye. "I'm as dumb as a donkey!" he cried.

"Bartholomew!" Nathan gasped. "What is it?"

"The woman! The pregnant woman! I was right there next to her . . ."

Bartholomew stopped to think, but Nathan was still confused. "Whatever are you talking about, boy?"

"I met the mother of the Messiah earlier tonight! At the inn of Hasrah!"

Seeing that his friend had no idea what he was talking about, Bartholomew pulled him by the arm and said, "Come on!" He turned and ran down the hill, followed by Nathan, who figured he'd better see what the boy was babbling about.

Below him, Bartholomew could see that Jotham, too, was running toward Bethlehem, with his entire clan following him. They would get there first, Bartholomew calculated, and so he forced his legs to move faster. Behind him he heard Nathan shouting, "Slow down, boy! You'll run straight out of your tunic!"

But Bartholomew continued on, reaching the bottom of the valley, then starting up the other side again, toward the City of David. As he entered the tiny town he saw that the line of people following Jotham had slowed to a halt. They filled the streets from wall to wall, and he pushed his way through them.

Finally he neared the inn of Hasrah, and he saw that the line of Jotham's people led straight down a little dirt ramp to the stable below. All the people were crowding to see. The travelers from inside the inn were pushing their way out as well, adding chaos to the confusion. It was then that Nathan caught up.

"Wha . . . what are we doing?" Nathan panted.

"The Messiah!" Bartholomew exclaimed, searching for a path through the crowd. "He has been born here!"

"What makes you think that?"

"Because," Bartholomew said, as if Nathan had asked the dumbest question in the world, "the angel said that we would find the baby . . ."

Bartholomew stopped talking, and Nathan looked over at him. "Find the baby *what*?" he asked. Bartholomew didn't answer. He was staring at the crowd of people pushing their way out of Hasrah's inn, and he looked as if he were seeing another angel. He didn't speak, didn't move, and Nathan wasn't even sure he was breathing. "Bartholomew," he said, "what is it?"

Bartholomew didn't answer and instead stumbled forward on shaky feet. He shuffled toward the inn, not taking his eyes off the people on its porch. He reached the bottom of the short staircase leading up to the inn and stood there, oblivious to the crowd pushing past him. Nathan came up next to him and noticed that he was staring at a boy of about fourteen—a boy of about fourteen who looked remarkably like Bartholomew.

"Jethro?" Bartholomew said under his breath. Then again more loudly he called, "Jethro!"

The boy looked up, and all the questions in the world crossed his face. Then the answer finally hit, and he called out, "Brother!"

In a flash the boy stuck his head back through the door to the inn and yelled something, and seconds later a man Bartholomew thought he'd never see again shot out the door, his eyes frantically searching through the crowd.

"Father!" Bartholomew yelled, and then the man spotted him. "Father!" he yelled again, and Bartholomew's father leaped the porch railing, ran the few steps to Bartholomew, and scooped his son up in his arms.

"My son, my son!" his father wept as he hugged Bartholomew close. "I feared we'd never find you again."

Moments later there was a shriek from the doorway, and Bartholomew's mother flew down the steps of the porch, followed by his brothers and sisters. All the family gathered around Bartholomew, all trying to hug him at the same time until he felt as if his insides would be squeezed out. But Bartholomew didn't care. His father's scratchy beard and the soft skin of his mother's face felt so good on his cheeks.

For many moments the family hugged and cried and laughed together, until finally Bartholomew asked through his tears, "Where have you been?"

Still holding his son, Bartholomew's father sat down on a low railing used to tie up camels. His mother and brothers and sisters all crowded around them.

"When the Romans attacked Taricheae," his father began, "we headed straight for home. But I sent Jethro to warn you and take you away from town."

"I got only as far as the cheese seller's booth," Jethro added, "before a Roman grabbed me by the neck."

"The rest of us were getting ready to flee," his father continued, "but a squad of soldiers broke down our door and captured us. We were all sent immediately to Joppa, where we were loaded onto ships. They were taking us to Rome to be slaves for a building project there."

"But we prayed to Jehovah," Bartholomew's mother picked up the story, "and He sent a great storm the next day." Bartholomew thought back on that day and remembered the storm that had made his own road to Caesarea so slippery. "Our ship was thrown onto the shore and broke apart, injuring all the Roman guards."

"So you took their swords and ran away?" Bartholomew guessed. His father smiled and shook his head slowly. Then another voice spoke up, from outside the family circle.

"No, Bartholomew," Nathan said, searching the lines on the face of Bartholomew's father and reading there the rest of the story. "They stayed and helped the wounded soldiers, treating their injuries, making hot soup for them, keeping them warm and dry until help arrived."

Bartholomew looked back and forth from Nathan to his father, his eyes questioning. His father nodded slowly and smiled. "This wise man is correct, Bartholomew," he said, "although how he could divine such a thing I do not understand."

"That's simple," Nathan said. "I know that the man who raised the boy Bartholomew could only be a good and decent and peaceful man, a man after Jehovah's own heart. And such a man would never turn his back on someone in need, be he Roman, Jew, or anyone else."

Bartholomew's father dropped his gaze to the ground in humble acceptance of the kind words, and Bartholomew finally understood. He introduced his two fathers to each other, and Bartholomew's real father and mother gave many thanks to Nathan.

"But how did you ever get away?" Bartholomew asked.

"We didn't," his father answered. "We were released. All of the other prisoners from the ship were eventually captured by Romans in the nearby towns. But the centurion of the squad that we helped let us go."

At this Jethro spoke up again. "He said that any man who would save the life of a bleeding enemy instead of taking care of himself must have a powerful faith in his God and didn't deserve to be a slave to anyone."

Bartholomew's father nodded the truth of the words, then added, "He gave us papers declaring that we are all free, and neither we nor any of our descendants can ever be made slaves again."

"And so we've been searching for you ever since," Bartholomew's mother completed the story. "We heard that the rest of our people were taken to Caesarea, and we were on our way there when we stopped at this inn for the night."

Suddenly Bartholomew remembered his own purpose for being in Bethlehem and jumped to his feet. "Come on!" he said, pulling his father's hand. "You've got to see this!"

Bartholomew's mother and father looked at each other, wondering what was happening, but they weren't about to lose sight of the son they had just found.

The crowd of people who had witnessed the reunion of Bartholomew's family parted ways so Bartholomew could lead his family to the front of the line. Bartholomew pushed his way inside the stable, which was small and dark and lit only by a single lamp. Then he saw his friend Jotham holding a tiny little baby, much smaller than a lamb. Jotham was showing the baby to his parents and family. On seeing his friend, Jotham cried out, "Bartholomew!"

"Greetings, my friend," Bartholomew grinned.

Jotham looked to the baby's mother for approval, then said, "Would you like to hold him?"

"Most assuredly!" Bartholomew answered. And so Jotham placed the child in his friend's arms.

The baby kicked a little under the swaddling cloth . . . let out a short cry, but then began cooing as Bartholomew held Him snugly against his chest. Then looking up at his family, and to Nathan who just then joined them, he said, "Mother, Father, I would like you to meet Jesus, the Messiah, . . . the Son of God!"

For unto *you* is born a Savior, Christ the Lord, who came to earth to tell you, and show you, and help you believe, the great and selfless love God has for you.

Merry Christmas!

Advent Through the Years

The following chart gives the Sunday on which Advent begins and the day of the week on which Christmas Eve falls, for the next several decades:

Year	Advent begins	Christmas Eve is	Year	Advent begins	Christmas Eve is	Year	Advent begins	Christmas Eve is
2009	November 29	Thursday	2033	November 27	Saturday	2057	December 2	Monday
2010	November 28	Friday	2034	December 3	Sunday	2058	December 1	Tuesday
2011	November 27	Saturday	2035	December 2	Monday	2059	November 30	Wednesday
2012	December 2	Monday	2036	November 30	Wednesday	2060	November 28	Friday
2013	December 1	Tuesday	2037	November 29	Thursday	2061	November 27	Saturday
2014	November 30	Wednesday	2038	November 28	Friday	2062	December 3	Sunday
2015	November 29	Thursday	2039	November 27	Saturday	2063	December 2	Monday
2016	November 27	Saturday	2040	December 2	Monday	2064	November 30	Wednesday
2017	December 3	Sunday	2041	December 1	Tuesday	2065	November 29	Thursday
2018	December 2	Monday	2042	November 30	Wednesday	2066	November 28	Friday
2019	December 1	Tuesday	2043	November 29	Thursday	2067	November 27	Saturday
2020	November 29	Thursday	2044	November 27	Saturday	2068	December 2	Monday
2021	November 28	Friday	2045	December 3	Sunday	2069	December 1	Tuesday
2022	November 27	Saturday	2046	December 2	Monday	2070	November 30	Wednesday
2023	December 3	Sunday	2047	December 1	Tuesday	2071	November 29	Thursday
2024	December 1	Tuesday	2048	November 29	Thursday	2072	November 27	Saturday
2025	November 30	Wednesday	2049	November 28	Friday	2073	December 3	Sunday
2026	November 29	Thursday	2050	November 27	Saturday	2074	December 2	Monday
2027	November 28	Friday	2051	December 3	Sunday	2075	December 1	Tuesday
2028	December 3	Sunday	2052	December 1	Tuesday	2076	November 29	Thursday
2029	December 2	Monday	2053	November 30	Wednesday	2077	November 28	Friday
2030	December 1	Tuesday	2054	November 29	Thursday	2078	November 27	Saturday
2031	November 30	Wednesday	2055	November 28	Friday	2079	December 3	Sunday
2032	November 28	Friday	2056	December 3	Sunday	2080	December 2	Monday

Also from Master Storyteller Arnold Ytreeide

O ver and over Jotham screamed for his family, but there was no one to hear him. They had vanished. He was alone. Where had they gone? How long ago did they leave? Through quick, stabbing sobs Jotham told himself, "I must look for my family. I must search until I find them." And so his journey began.

If you liked *Bartholomew's Passage,* don't miss *Jotham's Journey,* another charming Advent story to read with your whole family!